STILL
HERE

By

ELSA KURT

STILL HERE

Copyright © 2017 Elsa Kurt
All rights reserved.
ISBN: 197614177X
ISBN-13: 978-1976141775

ELSA KURT

DEDICATION

This book is dedicated to my husband, my always.

ACKNOWLEDGMENTS

With gratitude to my husband for his unwavering support, I can't do any of this without you. To my editing 'team'— Jennifer Petrozza, Mary Ellen Zenzie, Carol Hunsinger, and Lieza Bradshaw. Thank you for catching my mistakes! Every book is written to a soundtrack, the music sets the mood and sentiment as I write, so several of these songs found a way into the book via chapter quotes. Thank you to The Lone Bellow, Ingrid Michaelson, David Bowie, Journey, Ella Fitzgerald, David Gray, and Joe Cocker for making music that stirs my soul. Greats such as C.S. Lewis, Ernest Hemingway, Jane Austen, Robert Frost, Richard Bach, and Shakespeare, all added depth to the story via quotes. To anyone past and present who have inspired me, thank you.

CONTENTS

UNDERWATER	1
GRIEF ABOUNDING	7
BOTTOMLESS	15
HAPPY ANNIVERSARY	26
HEMINGWAY & AUSTEN	36
HOME BY THE SEA	41
WHISPERS	49
OLD FRIENDS	54
A CHANGE	78
LIMBO	83
RAGE	97
REAL	122
QUESTIONS	129
STAGES	142
SUNRISE	156
TUMAU	160
CAGES	168
AZRAEL	173
BLUEPRINTS	182
SCARS	194
JUMP	200
FLY	205

STILL HERE

ONE

UNDERWATER

"Oh, time won't you stay/ you're all I've got left/ I'm a man on my knees/ begging you please…"
—Time's Always Leaving, The Lone Bellow

"Don't be scared, lady. I've done it a bunch of times."

The boy couldn't be more than twelve. *Twelve.* And he's cliff dived 'a bunch of times.' I'm thirty-seven, and I've never jumped off a cliff. Nor have I ever wanted to until now. I mean, I still don't *want* to, but for Damon, I will.

"Thanks, kid. It's that obvious, huh?"

"It's okay, lots of people are scared. It's your time, though."

Cold sweat prickles in the pits of my arms, gooseflesh rises on my skin. My stomach tightens and tremors ripple through my body like electric currents. I don't think I've ever been this scared before. Before I can respond, he speaks again.

"We can jump together if you want. But first, tell me your name, miss."

I finally turn my head from the impossibly far away blue-green water, and down at the sweet child beside me. A perfect stranger. His eyes are amber, his young skin—the color of warm cocoa—hugs his jutting bones. Water droplets sparkle in his tight curls like diamonds in the sun. He's so calm.

A little laugh escapes through my chattering teeth. Not at the boy, but at myself. I draw in a shaky breath and nod on the exhale. My hand flutters to my chest, and I press my palm hard against the violent drumming beneath my breast, as if I could quell it.

Less than thirty minutes earlier, I said I would try it, though. That was before I looked over the ledge, down at the sea so far below.

"Just once," Damon had promised from right beside me, where the boy is now.

"You'll be so glad you did it, Birdie."

He counted to three and jumped. I let go of his hand at the last second and drew back as he launched forward. Regret and relief tangled inside me as I watched my husband sail through the air. The breath I'd been holding sighed out of my lips the moment he broke the surface and shouted something unintelligible up to me. But knowing Damon as I do, it was no doubt some words of encouragement. He's down there now. Still waiting patiently for me to find my courage.

I purse my lips together in a grim white line. Blood rushes and thumps in my ears. I hear my own voice as if through a windstorm.

STILL HERE

"It's Birdie. Birdie Harrison."

The boy smiles up at me as he leans in.

"I'll count to three, and then we'll jump. Ready?"

I nod this time; slower, more deliberate. My heart is thudding like a bass drum keeping time for an invisible band.

"One....
 Two...
  Three..."

The boy whose name I don't know—whose skin is like warm cocoa, eyes the color ochre, and hair that is diamond jeweled—swan jumps. My feet do an awkward shuffle, my knees bend. But I don't so much leap as *fall* forward. Air rushes past my ears, and my hair whips around my face before it streams behind me like ribbons of pale fire. Everything is a blur. Except for the boy, that is.

He does a slow backflip in the air, and time slows as his round, calm eyes meet mine. My heart isn't thundering anymore. There are only the eyes of the boy, the wind, and the blue-green lagoon far (so very far) away. And Damon, of course. My sweet Damon.

His name in my head starts the clock again, and my eyes widen then squeeze shut at the immediacy of impact. My head and shoulders plunge into the cold water like a rocket. Though the surface is an inviting shade of teal, it has belied a twilight blue underbelly.

Straight down I go, for what seems like forever. At last, my momentum slows, and I can turn myself toward the surface. Underwater, everything is a muted. A murmuring quiet but for the sound of blurps and blubs of the under-ocean. My eyes are open again. Minuscule particles fleck the dense scene like lazy snowflakes. My breath, held in against the water, strains to restart.

I need to breathe, to get back to the surface.

Swaying tendrils of hair dance in from my face. I sweep them aside in slow-motion and blink up towards the surface. It seems so far away. I scissor-kick and push the dense water down with my arms. The sunlight refracts the water's uppermost layer. The dizzying ripples of water and light are so close, yet so far. But no matter how hard I kick and push, it seems to not be getting closer.

Air. I need to pull air into my lungs. I know this logically, but why is there no pressure inside my chest? No tight, fiery burn from my strained diaphragm? One part of my brain wonders at this, the other panics. *I'm going to drown, my God, I'm going to drown.*

Breathing is a reflex, no matter how hard you fight it, your body will insist upon it. So, with at least twenty feet of water between me and the surface, my panicked brain tells me to inhale. I gasp involuntary and pull in salty water. First through my nose—a tickling trickle. Then—when it doesn't sting or burn as I'd anticipated, I open my mouth, thirsty for oxygen, yet I am breathing water.

I can breathe underwater. Oh, my God. I can't wait to tell Damon.

All those years of strange recurring nightmares of drowning, a waste of precious sleep. I don't question the impossibility of this. Not when Damon is mere feet away now, and he will be so amazed at my discovery.

My legs kick and push me upward, through the dense water. A broad smile spreads across my face as I picture Damon at the surface. I imagine him waiting with pride in his soulful eyes at his brave wife. I giggle a little bit, sending a flurry of bubbles from my nose.

Just as I finally near the sunlight dappled layer, a sturdy pair of arms reach down and grab me hard under my armpits. Damon's hands, I'd know them anywhere. But why would he pull me so crudely? My head breaks the surface, and I gasp again. This time, air replaces the water, as if it were the most natural occurrence. Another fabulous marvel!

I blink and find myself supine on a sun-warmed boulder, Damon's beautiful face hovering above me. His deep brown eyes look wild as they search my face, for what, I don't know. Saltwater drips from his long dark curls onto my skin. Tap, tap, tap. My God, he looks as if he's staring death in the face.

Fear and worry have drained the color from his suntanned skin. The corners of his perfect mouth are pulled down, his strong chin shakes. My brow furrows and then smooths as I try to smile at him, show him I'm fine. I need to take away that look on his face, my poor man.

"I'm perfectly fine, babe."

That's what I say, but I can't hear myself over the sound of rushing wind in my ears. It's like I'm still falling through the air. I try again, this time straining my vocal cords.

"Damon, I'm fine, really."

It's like being on mute. Another couple is beside Damon. The woman has a heart-shaped face and wears one of those two-piece floral print bathing suits. The kind heavier-set women in their fifties tend to favor. She puts a chubby hand on his bare shoulder. The man shouts in an accented bellow voice, 'Medic! We need a medic!' across the lagoon to the bystanders on the beach. Everyone seems frantic.

Everyone but me… and the beautiful brown boy with the striking eyes. He has my hand in both of his, head bowed, and he is speaking low. He's praying.

"Hey! Kid. What's happening? Am I—am I hurt? I don't feel hurt…"

The boy's head comes up, his doleful eyes lock on mine, and he shakes it slowly. Before I can say anything more, Damon pulls me into his arms, hard against his chest. He smells like sun and sea and men's deodorant. He rocks, his strong arms enveloping me as if I am but a small child, and speaks only one word —

"No, no, no, no, no…"

It becomes a long, bottomless moan of grief. A chill runs through me. Now I understand.

TWO
GRIEF ABOUNDING

There's sorrow in your voice, it's abounding It's astounding how you live so close to your cure
—Let Go, Ingrid Michaelson

Grief. Once, several years ago, a friend of mine gave the eulogy at his father's funeral. He read a quote: 'grief is the price we pay for profound love.' I'd been fidgeting, twisting my rings, my hair, the hem of my dress, shifting in the hard, wooden pew, until I heard that line. *Grief is the price we pay for profound love.* A current of electricity shot up my spine. Oh, the depth of those words. Words have always had this kind of power over me. So moved I was by the line, that I obsessed over it. I looked for opportunities to use it, reciting it at any appropriate moment. There have been so many appropriate moments, I'm saddened to say.

Grief. Profound. Love.

Oh, these words together are almost too much to bear. Profound grief. Profound love. Yes, hand in hand they go. Mustn't they? They beg the question: Should we love deeply despite the fear of loss? Before Damon, I'd have said no, but because of him, I say *yes, of course*. I say now and always, *yes*. I would willingly pay the price for this kind of love, mine and Damon's. Were things reversed—if it were Damon's lifeless body on the rocks of an island lagoon instead of mine—I would accept grief as the cost of the love we had. *Have*. Love like ours can't die; I'm living (well dead, technically) proof of it.

Honestly? I don't know what's going on. I'm still trying to understand it. I mean, I'm dead, that much is for certain. The autopsy said I died before I even hit the water. My heart just... stopped. *Hypertrophic Cardiomyopathy*. Genetic, possibly. The pathologist suggested my parents have my siblings tested. There are no siblings; there is only me, so that's not a concern.

The local paper gave it a front-page nod, above the fold, mind you. "Local Woman Dies Tragically in Cliff Diving Accident." Typical. They couldn't even get the headline right. *Accident*. It wasn't an accident that killed me, it was my covertly defective heart that did me in. The headline *should've* been, "Local Woman's Fucked Up Heart Kills Her in Prime of Her Life."

Sorry. I'm just trying to lighten up the mood here, I know it's all awful. Snarky humor has always been my go-to when things get too serious. And this shit, it is *serious*. Why, if I weren't already dead, it would kill me to see what my family is going through. See, I can't help myself; it just comes out.

It used to drive Damon a little crazy when I'd—as he called it—*shut down emotionally* like that. But he knows that even though I'm terrible at *saying* my feelings, I'm also kind of great (if I do say so myself) at writing them. Usually. Or, *used to be*. Death has knocked that talent out of me, it seems.

Damon. Now that knocks the funny right out of me. My poor Damon, with his dark circles under his eyes, unshaven face, and nightly pacing. How he is suffering right now. I'm half convinced it's why I'm still here, in this in-between. At least, that's what all those life-after-death movies and books have led me to believe. Who'd have thought it was real, this whole ghost-with-unfinished-business stuff?

Confession? I'm stalling. I don't want to talk about Damon, the Damon of right now. It's too much. His big, puppy eyes look hollow, vacant. He hardly eats. My throat catches at his every flinch at the mention of my name. Every fist curl at the sound of audacious laughter in his presence.

The steady outpouring of sympathies and regrets are salt to his wound. I can't comfort him. Watching him hurt is like a thousand razorblades cutting at my soul. So, please, let me ease my way in, okay? We'll start here, where the recalling is easy…

…

I grew up like most girls. Fairytales and princes, knight-in-shining-armor, you know, *the usual.* I loved it all, still do. Even as a dead woman. In my defective heart of hearts, I *knew* there was a prince out there for me. I knew it the way you know your own damn name. *Absolute certainty.* Sure, there were a few toads along the way. Okay, fine, a lot of toads. Two false princes, too. But I wasn't giving up. I'm no quitter, people.

My mother would say, "Sweetheart, get your head out of the clouds. There's just no such thing as the perfect man. Except for your father, of course."

Eye roll, a nod to eavesdropping husband.

"If you've got one who's honest and loyal, kind and hardworking, be happy," she finished with a self-satisfied nod.

My father would say, "Peach, ya gotta accept us for how we are, and we aren't complex creatures. Beer. Football. Food. And some stuff your mother can talk to you about."

Their words belied their mutual happiness in marriage. They have an admirable love, but it wasn't quite what *I* had in mind for me. They are textbook, I wanted storybook. They thought I was looking for the perfect man, but I was looking for the perfect man *for me*.

When I was thirty-two, I met Damon. Damon Michael Harrison, my perfect for me. We met in a bookstore, between two alphabetically organized bookshelves of Classic Literature. I held Jane Austen in my hand as if it were the Holy Grail, he had Hemingway pressed to his nose, eyes closed. I could tell by the creases at the corners of his eyes; he was smiling. My heart—the flawed thing it is...*was*—swelled at the sight of a man loving a book so much he had to inhale it.

"Will you be tracking it later?"

It was a stupid thing to say—to suggest he was a hunting dog—but he opened his eyes and smiled.

"No need. This little leather-bound beast is coming home with me."

"Hemingway, hmm?"

He made to steal a look at the title tucked behind my arm, and I obliged him.

"Jane Austen, hmm? What do suppose they'd say to each other if they ever could've met?"

"I can't imagine. But I'd love to be a fly on the wall for it."

"Me, too. Have coffee with me."

If another man had presented an invitation as a command, I'd laugh in his face. But the way Damon said it, well, it was different. Somehow, it was all things at once—statement, question, command. It didn't hurt *at all* that he had big puppy-brown, brooding eyes, eyelashes that'd make any girl jealous. Not to mention his men's magazine-worthy tousled chestnut locks. Or that he had the build of a fitness model, or... okay, I found him to be quite pleasing to the eye. So, I said yes to his non-question.

We sat at a small bistro table in the corner of the quiet bookstore. Ordered strong hazelnut coffee. We even shared a crumbly orange-cranberry scone, the last one in the case. Etta James voice poured from the speakers like raw honey. We discussed our favorite authors, movies, songs, our favorite everythings. Errands and obligations went out the window, time was forgotten. It was simple, easily justified. You see, we fell in love across that scarred table.

A young girl tasked with shooing us out of the building approached. Her myopic eyes locked on Damon as if he were Adonis incarnate. He handed her a twenty-dollar bill and a slow smile and asked for fifteen more minutes. Her eyes darted about the store, then she nodded before disappearing again.

"Twenty bucks for fifteen minutes? We could've taken this conversation across the street to the bar, you know. May have cost you less."

Damon leaned forward, as did I, and slid his fingers across the small table to mine. When our fingertips touched, he pushed mine up, so that our hands lifted and pressed against each other. We looked like we were taking a pledge, I'm sure. Then, with an adorably solemn expression, he stated,

"I wanted just a little more time in the place we'll be remembering as the beginning of our love story."

He *really* said that, my Damon. Always the romantic. It was never contrived with him, either. I've had so-called romantic lines tossed at me in my life, and to my ears, they always sounded practiced and fake. But Damon was the anomaly in a world of cliché men. As for me? Well, I was always his comedic foil.

"Interesting love story that'll be. We don't know each other's names, even."

He smiled *that smile*— the one I'd swear could melt polar ice caps in an instant, and said,

"Damon Michael Harrison."

"Birdie Taylor Tenley. No one calls me Birdie, though. That was my great-great grandmother's name. It's just Taylor."

"Then I want to call you Birdie. If that's alright with you?"

I squinted at him a moment, a goofy grin plastered on my face. I always found the name to be embarrassing, silly, and antiquated. Maybe once upon a time, it was charming or endearing, but I'd never thought it suited me. I'm neither fragile nor delicate, even if I am small. But from Damon's lips, it sounded right. Plus, I simply couldn't say no to that face. And so, from that day forward, I was his Birdie. I *am* his Birdie.

There's only one way I can describe Damon's entrance into my life. It's like this: In the movie version of The Wizard of Oz, there's that moment after Dorothy's house lands in Munchkin land. She opens the door, and magically everything is in Technicolor. Gone is the dull sepia tone of her existence. Damon is like *that*. Red is redder; blue is deeper, yellow is sunnier, green is more vibrant. At the beginning of us, it was almost too much to bear, the intensity of his being.

My pastel previous life could not compete with the riot of primary color of his. Once I'd seen what his world looked like... well, unlike Dorothy, I didn't want ever to go back home. So, I jumped.

Ah, I guess that's not such a good metaphor for me anymore, is it? But that's how I recall it, a leap of inexplicable faith in a man I'd met over Hemingway and coffee.

I'm *supposed* to say here that, hey, we've had our share of ups and downs these five years. But I won't lie to you. Not now, when I'm too dead to care if you roll your eyes and say, '*yeah sure.*' Our life has been one long, happily-ever-after of a fairy tale. A modern day one, of course. No dragons, queens, castles, and whatnot. Just a man and a woman, profoundly, intensely, wholly in love with one another, with our *life* together. Boring, right?

I want to keep telling you this part, the good stuff. The happy stuff. The easy stories and memories that only bring smiles to my lips. But I am watching Damon now, *right now*, and I… well, I need a moment.

THREE
BOTTOMLESS

It's only forever. Not long at all.
—Jareth, Labyrinth

Dead people should not be able to have headaches. But I do. My head *hurts*. My heart, that traitorous bitch, it hurts too. I'm trying so hard to find a way into his consciousness. So many times, I've tried.

"Oh, Damon. If you could just try, try to hear me. Feel me; I'm right *here* beside you. Don't you feel my lips tickling your ear?"

Nothing.

Sometimes, I tuck my nose—the one I always said is too long, and he said is just right for me—into his curls, inhaling the clean smell of his shampoo. Or, I rest my hand on his chest as it rises and falls, his heartbeat steady against my palm. I breathe in his scent when he brushes by me, unaware of my nearness.

"I can smell you; I can *feel* you, damn it. Why can't you sense me? Let me take this agony from you. Please."

It is to no avail. This is cruel. I'm telling you, this is unfair and wickedly cruel. To let Danon suffer, to make me watch, helpless. Damn you, whoever you are. God? No, I don't accept a cruel God. *My* God would never tear at us so. *My* God is love; I'll believe nothing less.

Damon always accepted my strange faith as is. It's one that refuses religion but has boundless trust in spiritualism. As for Damon, he believes without a doubt there is something greater than us. He said once:

"All I can say for sure is, I have faith. There's something *more*, I know it. I like your ideas, Birdie. It's very sweet and exactly why I love you. Your heart is like endless miles and bottomless depths."

My poet, my Damon. He's the better writer of us two. He is the lyrics to my melodies, the words to my blank pages. Everything I can never say with any semblance of ease—he sees and says it all with effortless comfort. So, why can he not hear me now? Death should be no match for him. Not for Damon Michael Harrison.

I guess I can't hide behind lofty allusions, memories, and pithy words anymore, it's unjust. It's time again to be in the now, no matter how painful it is to watch. We'll watch together until I figure out how to reach him.

...

"Damon? It's me, Claire. I'm coming in, dear."

STILL HERE

Damon doesn't answer. He continues staring out the bay window, watching the white-tipped waves roll in. I lean against the window frame, my arms crossed over my chest, and take in his melancholy profile. When the wide front door opens, carrying the musical sound of a woman's voice, I turn, but he does not. Not at first. It's my mother, come again to check on him.

He squeezes his eyes shut at the sound of her voice; it's the older, modulated version of mine. He clutches the window frame in one hand. The other hand presses between his eyes, then he rakes his hair back, blowing out a slow, heavy breath.

I know what he sees when he looks at her. It is like seeing his Birdie of the future; only there will *be* no Birdie in his future. Damon's nostrils flare as he inhales and loosens his grip, visibly willing himself to be steady, be still.

"There you are. Right where I left you yesterday. Damon, you…"

"Thank you for coming, Claire. You really don't need to keep checking on me. I'm dealing…"

"Nonsense, Damon, you're like a son to us. Taylor would…"

Claire chokes back a sob.

"I'm sorry, they—it just sneaks up on me like that sometimes. I don't even have to be talking about her… *Taylor*. It could be the weather, or tennis, anything really. And there it is, this mean, unbidden whisper in my head, *'childless mother.'* It's like a slap in the face. I…"

She wrings her hands. Takes birdlike steps to the kitchen entrance, then back again to the living room. Her hands rise and drop again, and she continues, haltingly.

"It's just—who am I now? If not Claire, wife of Thomas Tenley, mother of Birdie Taylor Tenley-Harrison? Thomas is drowning in his despair, he can't help..."

She stops, takes a shaky breath. Straightens her spine and smooths her cream-colored pencil skirt. Damon moved towards her, his arms outstretched, but she lifts a delicate, manicured hand and shakes her head firmly.

"Not that I need help, dear. The only thing that can help me is helping *you*. And Thomas, of course. I need... I need to be *useful*. However, if I—if I'm bothering you, or intruding, just..."

"You're no bother, Claire. None at all. Really."

The hard edge has left his tone; his face has softened. He has stepped outside of his grief for a moment to appreciate hers. Sweet man. Even in pain, he is gracious. *Both* of them, so gracious. They are more alike than I ever before realized.

My mother has always seen this in Damon, his deep well of compassion for others. She knows his story, his unspoken need for mothering. Loving my Damon as if he were her own came as naturally to her as breathing. She loves him the way a boy needs to be loved by a mother. I've never been more grateful to her than I am right now.

I watch her now, my beautiful mother. Always the essence of real refinement and is no different now. An elegant woman of restraint and tact; diminutive in size but mighty in presence. Her pale, salon-coiffed hair frames her petite, angular face.

Her dark blue eyes have always conveyed both warmth and confidence. Her posture, despite her anguish, is still ruler straight. Like a blonde Audrey Hepburn. Now, though no less elegant, loss and sorrow have faded her. She is still Claire, but she is something else now, too. She is changed. They all are.

As for Damon, he's aged a decade in a month's time. New grey hairs seemed to have appeared overnight, scattered along his temples. He's lost weight, enough for it to make his face look harder, older. The lines at the corners of his eyes, across his brow, are etched deeper.

Claire takes a sharp breath through her nose, releases it, and nods her head to some internal dialogue. She appraises him anew with her cerulean eyes.

"I know how deeply you loved our girl. More importantly, *Taylor* knew it as well, dear. I—I just want you always to know that."

She is right, of course. I've never doubted his love. Damon is a man *impossible* to doubt, no matter how unbelievable it seems for him to be real. He is a man whose sincerity is impossible to distrust. Whose eyes bore into your soul with intensity and earnestness. Whose smile can thaw icebergs. Whose laughter could spread across a room like a wave. He is simply exceptional.

Daddy used to tease me about him often.

"Peach, you're gonna break that poor boy's heart one day, I just know it," he'd laugh. "He's too fragile for a little bull like you!"

"Oh, Daddy, stop it! I love him; I am *not* going to break his heart, now or ever. Anyhow, he's the *least* fragile person I've ever known. Aside from you, of course. Besides, aren't you supposed to be warning *him* not to break *my* heart?"

"Okay, okay, Peach. You're right, fragile wasn't the right word. But, I still think you're gonna break that boy's heart, kiddo."

I protested more, much to my father's amusement. In the end, though, he was right. I *have* broken his heart now, haven't I? As my gaze shifts from Damon to my mother, a sharp pain writhes in my stomach. I've broken all their hearts.

Damon knew Claire had needed a moment to compose herself. She doesn't like showing vulnerability, just like her daughter. We do not like to appear weak. It's a Tenley women thing, I suppose. Tears are for private, and never in front of others.

We'd been together for a year when I finally allowed Damon to see me cry. My beloved Shepherd, Maximillian had reached the end of his days.

"Sixteen years, that's a great run for a large dog," announced the vet, not unsympathetically.

It *was* a very good run, for a very good dog. It didn't lessen the hollow ache in my chest at saying goodbye. It didn't soften my grief.

Damon speaks to Claire, rousing me from my reverie. It's as though he hears my thoughts subconsciously.

STILL HERE

"I keep thinking about that damn line, '*grief is the price we pay for profound love.*' Birdie used to say that a lot. She—"

"—was obsessed with it," Claire finishes with a grim smile. They know me so well.

Damon nods, the start of a smile claims half his mouth but then drops away.

"Now it's stuck in my head. Like a damn broken record, it's her voice, in my head. I just—Jesus, Claire. Is it ever going to not hurt?"

Claire remains quiet; it is the most Damon has spoken to anyone since the day I died. Her hand flutters to and presses against her chest.

"That phone call... it is a scar I think I will wear across my heart always. I remember I dropped the phone; it just fell from my hand to the counter. I—I knew. A mother knows."

Clair looks down at her hand, as if seeing the phantom phone, and hears Damon's voice in her mind. Her face is wan, stricken once again as she relives the memory. The rest, I recall.

I hovered beside them all unseen. Damon carried me with painstaking care over the rocks to the beach, refusing all help. An ambulance awaited, its siren silent and emergency lights lit. Bystanders openly gawked, some had the decency to avert their eyes when Damon's met them. It didn't matter; he saw none of them. Then we were driven to the dock, where a boat waited, motor running. It carried a plain-clothed police officer assigned to interviewing Damon across the ocean, from the island to the mainland and us. Another ambulance met us there. Its lights and sirens, too, were still and quiet as it transported us through the town to a small hospital. No one spoke more than a few words to Damon, respecting his shock and self-imposed isolation. I watched Damon the whole time; we were both in shock, I suppose.

Later, my poor mother and father would race hand in hand through the emergency entrance doors. The room where they'd put my body was just around the corner of the front desk. We could hear their footsteps as they approached.

My mother breaks our respective reveries.

"The whole world had lost its hue, but you, Damon Michael Harrison, you were somehow still in color. You know, Taylor said once, when you first started dating—you were like *'Technicolor in a sepia world.'*" I smile through my tears when she says, "I—I couldn't take my eyes off you."

She doesn't have to say what she's thinking, I know. If she did, she must look at the still form in the hospital bed where Damon's gaze remained locked. She had stepped into the darkened room, Daddy close behind, his big hand heavy and firm on her shoulder. The clack of her heels roused Damon. He turned his head towards them, peeling his eyes from what lies on the bed. At the sight of his surrogate mother, he let out all he'd been holding in.

"I — she... it's my fault, Claire. It's my fault. I..."

Her son-in-law's torment had been enough to mobilize her. She would have none of that because her daughter would've had none of that. Later, she will say she could almost feel my spirit rise around her, and hear my voice say, *'protect him from himself, Mom. Please.'*

"Come here, sweetheart. Come to Mom."

She rushed to Damon, avoiding looking at the bed still, and cupped his elbows, compelling him to her.

"You are every bit my son, our *family*, and I'll not leave you to be devoured by grief and guilt, do you hear?"

He cried like a child on her shoulder. Wracking, soul-crushing sobs of a man whose everything was gone. Daddy had remained in the doorway, ashen and stricken.

"Thomas. Come, take our boy out into the hallway. I need some time with my baby."

Daddy walked halfway into the room, and Claire pushed Damon gently to him. When Damon resisted, unwilling to leave his wife, Claire was firm.

"*Now*, gentlemen. Give me my time with my girl."

So, the two men, opposite in every way, but united by a profound love, walked arm and arm out into the quiet corridor. Claire waited until they rounded the corner before pulling Damon's vacated chair up towards the head of the bed. She didn't sit, though. Instead, she smoothed the already smooth sheet over her child's legs. She rested a hand on my cold calf. The cold, the stillness... she pulled her hand away. At last, she looked up at my face.

"So still, so smooth... so beautiful. Like Princess Aurora in Sleeping Beauty," she whispered to no one.

"You got your prince after all, just as you always said you would."

Claire tried to smile, but her mouth quivered. Her eyes welled, and tears spilled onto the sheet as she stroked my cold cheek with her soft hand, and then she sighed. A small breath of air drifting from her trembling lips at first. But the air wouldn't stop leaving her body once it started. Her stomach sucked in; her chest caved, her body doubled over the bed, her baby.

"My baby, my baby..."

She gasped air and tears and strands of her only child's silky hair into her mouth. They tasted of sea salt. She gave in to her grief, but only for a moment. As quickly as she'd yielded, Claire composed herself. She straightened, smoothed my hair back into place, and flattened the sheets around my body as if tucking me in for the night. From her purse, she extracted a small compact and tissue.

"Our men will need a rock, Taylor, and I will be it. That's how Tenley women do things."

She snapped the compact closed.

"Isn't that right, dear? I'll take care of them for you, sweetheart."

She sniffed, dabbed below each eye, continued,

"You hear me? I promise I'll take care of your Daddy *and* your prince."

The men returned. Daddy raised his shoulders and threw his hands out wide; his shrug is saying, 'I tried to keep him away, Claire.' Damon raced in as if someone may have stolen his wife away while he was out, then stopped short at the sight of the bed.

His wide-eyed gaze landed on my motionless body, still in eternal repose where he'd left me. His troubled brow and wild eyes calmed as he exhaled. Then he winced as if in physical pain and pressed his hands hard against his eyes as if reliving my death anew.

Poor thing, Claire's expression said, not for the first or last time. This was only the beginning of their new way of life.

FOUR
HAPPY ANNIVERSARY

Lonely rivers sigh — Wait for me, wait for me
I'll be comin' home, wait for me
—Unchained Melody, Righteous Brothers

Mom was right, you know. About everything. Specifically, though — she was right about hearing me in the hospital room that night. I *did* tell her to go to him, protect him from himself. Shocked the hell out of me.

"Yes! Mom, you heard me!"

Alas, not everything goes as smoothly as we want. I figured it'd be like that movie, Ghost. You know, the one where the wife makes pottery with her dead husband? In a nutshell: Patrick Swayze's character tries to find a way to make his grieving wife believe he was present. He finds a psychic who *can* hear him and makes her relay his message. Cue Unchained Melody for that epically romantic scene.

Obviously, there's more to the movie than that, and of course, it was super romantic.

I was so sure Mom would be *my* Oda Mae Brown, but after that dreadful day, no matter how hard I've tried, it hasn't worked again. Back to square one. There is no doubt in my mind; I will get to Damon. I *must*. Every night, while he tosses and turns, I pace the floor, trying to figure out how. Never do I stray further than the balcony or the den. I won't leave his side, though I'm pretty sure I can.

If you had seen him when I died, it would leave a scar on *your* heart. His face would flash before your eyes at unexpected moments. The memory of his expression when the dawning of understanding hit him in the chest. The sound of his voice saying *no*, over and over. Not being able to make him okay. It would break you. It breaks me.

As my pacing feet trace invisible tracks across the carpet, I contemplate all the possible ways to make him see me. A chant repeats over and over in my head:

I need to take his pain away. I need to take his pain away. I need to take his pain away.

I can't stand it. I can't bear being the source of Damon's agony. In my head, I hear my father's words, *'You'll break that boy's heart, Peach'* and a wave of nausea washes over me. He was right. I know this wasn't what he foresaw, of course, but here we are.

This comes out as a kind of arrogance, I realize, but I can say I've always been sure of Damon's love for me. I've known it in the same way you know everyday kind of things. The sun will come up.

Seasons change. Puppies are cute. Damon loves me. I got used to it. It stopped awing me at some point.

But the genuine depth of that love? The *wholeness* of it? No, not until I saw him grieve. His love for me, it buckles my knees. It humbles me. And now, I would rather a lifetime of just feeling *pretty sure* I'm loved than to have to see him grieve me. Yes, I am saying I would sacrifice my desire for great love if it could spare him this.

I once thought I could accept the consequence of extraordinary love. But that was when I naively and selfishly believed the consequence was only mine to suffer. It was before I comprehended grief's long reaching fingers and vast grasp. What I know now, is that I can take my sorrow, but not his. Not my poor Damon's.

Since the start of my newfound ghost status, there lurks the panic that I will disappear and squander this chance I've somehow been given. Here is what I've come to believe: *I am still here to help Damon.* I'm still here, not for me or my needs and wishes, but for *him.* He is the one who deserves a reprieve from mourning.

If ever there were a man worth waiting lifetimes for, it would be — it *is*— Damon Michael Harrison. He is all things good and right. The precisely right balance of strength and gentleness, flaws and perfections, sweetness and mischief. Am I biased? One could say if just hearing my list of qualities and attributes, that yes, bias is at play. I can't have that, have anyone doubt his greatness. So, yes, it has come time to show what being loved by Damon looks and feels like. Let's rewind and go back to *that* day.

...

Police Officer: Mr. and Mrs.— uh, Sommers, is it? Can you tell us what you saw happen today?"

Mr. Sommers: "Right, right. Name's Ian, and this my wife, Ruthie. Terrible business, that poor chap. I, well, let's see. I came upon the fellow, hear him say, '*C'mon, baby, I know you can do it,*' so I said to him, '*You think she'll jump?*' and he gave me a bit of a quick side-eye, then back up to his wife…"

Mrs. Sommers: "Yes, and that's when I called out to Ian, I said, 'I've your sunglasses right here, do you want them,' and then I looked up at how very high up that woman — his wife — was. I think I said, '*my that's quite high up, isn't it?*' Isn't that right, Ian?"

Mr. Sommers: "That's about right, love. Then I said, '*No, no Ruthie, you just sit tight, dear. Yes, it's high up, love.*' And then…"

Police Officer: "Sir, ma'am, I don't need every…"

Mr. Sommers: "I gave him the old, '*can't live with 'em, can't live without 'em* lines. Eh, regretting that about now, I am."

Police Officer: "And then what happened, sir?"

Mr. Sommers: "Well, let's see. The young man said, '*We were supposed to jump together. I counted to three, but…*' and I finished it for him 'cause I knew it, '*But she got scared, I suppose,*' is what I said to him. The chap nodded. No need to confirm the obvious, I suppose.

Police Officer: So, they did *not* jump together? I see. And then..."

Mr. Sommers: "Right, yes. Well, let's see. Oh, then he says, '*She's brave. Joins me on any adventure, even ones like this, that scare her.*' Then, quiet-like, I hear him say, '*Birdie is tough, she can do this.*' I thought..."

Mrs. Sommers: "Oh, Ian, I hadn't heard that part! Why it breaks my heart. Such a handsome young man. She's — was a beauty, too. Regular tragedy, it is."

Mr. Sommers: "Yes, that it is, love. Anyhow, he cupped his hands around his mouth, like this, he did, and he started to yell, '*You don't have to do it....*' We could hardly make her out, but for her red swimsuit. Just then, at that very moment, a cloud passed over the sun. It was like a foreboding, now I think, and she stood out brightly..."

Police Officer, sighing: "Sir..."

Mrs. Sommers: "Oh, I could see her well enough, love. You really should've had your sunglasses on, as I'd offered. *Anyhoo*— I could see her. She turned her head to the right—our right, that is—like she was looking down at something besides her. Then, she faced the water again. I watched her knees bend, and then suddenly—oh my goodness, she was falling through the air. *Falling*. It wasn't a jump, I tell you. My heart just sank, it did, when I saw that. I think we all knew it instantly. I heard you, Ian, say, '*Oh.*'"

STILL HERE

Mr. Sommers, his voice quavering: "Yes, that's right, Ruthie. You were on the rocks, and I heard you gasp. After what felt like an eternity, right Ruthie? She hit the water with a sickening clap, so close to the rocks that several people gasped."

Police Officer: "And who got to her first?"

Mr. Sommers: "Oh, that would be the husband, he got to her first. Fellow swam like sharks were after him, he did. Poor chap. Ruthie and I weren't far behind. I tried to help lift her, but he was frantic, *'No! I've got her. I've got her,'* he yelled. Terrible sound, it was, that man's voice, I'll never forget it as long as I live. Ruthie, you..."

Mrs. Sommers: "Yes, yes. Of course, dear. My poor husband, he's very shaken up. As am I. Why, if you'd heard him yourself, saying, *'Birdie. Birdie! Come on, baby. You're alright. You're alright...'* Tears your heart out, it does. He kept saying it, over and over, trying to make it so, but her body was limp, like a ragdoll, it was."

Police Officer: "Did anyone try to resuscitate the victim?"

"Mrs. Sommers: "Oh, my, yes! The husband. He tried his best, did it just like you see on the telly. Had his hands interlocked and pressing on her chest — her *sternum*. That's the right word. Then he put his mouth over hers, giving her his breath. I don't think he even knew it, but I had put a hand on his shoulder. It was clear to everyone but him she was gone. But, bless him, he said, *'No. Medics are coming; they'll bring her back. She'll be okay.'* To her, he just begged, *'Oh, God. Please, Birdie, wake up.'* Oh, bloody hell, now I need a tissue, too."

Police Officer, clearing his throat and blinking hard: "Thank you, both. If we, uh, have any further questions, we know where to find you."

The officer then walked over to Damon.

"Sir, I'll be escorting you to the dock where we'll have a boat ready to take you to the mainland."

Damon nodded but said nothing. His eyes were on me. Well, my lifeless body, that is.

"I'm going to be asking you some questions on the way, I apologize."

No response from Damon.

"Sir? I realize this is difficult, but I must ask them, and I need you to answer."

Damon dragged his gaze off the sheet covered gurney and to the plain-clothed officer.

"Fine. My wife is dead. What more do you want to know?"

His voice was almost unrecognizable to my ears, raw and monotonic. He looked through the officer with bloodshot eyes. His body shivered in waves; his hand trembled as he rubbed the back of his neck.

"Let's start with the moment you and your wife reached the cliff's edge. Was there anyone else up there with you?"

"No."

"And did you and your wife jump together?"

Damon shook his head, swallowed hard several times. His stare already returned to the gurney. Then, his voice raw, hoarse, he whispered, "I jumped first. We were supposed to jump together."

"Yes, you were."

"What?"

Damon turned his gaze back to the officer, a crease formed between his eyebrows. Mine, too.

"Nothing. I just meant—never mind. So, you jumped first and waited for your wife to jump. And was there anyone else with you?"

"You asked me that already. I *told* you, it was just us. I jumped, she didn't. I waited for her, the heavyset older man and his wife can attest."

"Yes, right. Sorry. The couple, can you describe them?"

"*Describe* them? Why? Just, fine they, uh, he was impossibly tan and had a shiny bald head. Big belly, sloped over those, um, Bermuda shorts. He was in the water, next to me. His wife, she had on a flowery, two-piece swimsuit. She was on the rocks. What the hell else do you want from me?"

"That'll be all. Thank you, and we're sorry...for your loss."

Damon gave a sharp nod, his face pale and stony.

"Here we are, at the dock. They'll transport you to the mainland. I hope... good luck, Mr. Harrison."

Everything after that went by in a blur. The boat ride. The hospital staff with their murmurs and kindness. All this happened, but like in a vacuum or a funnel. A swirling blend of sights and sounds, like we're in the eye of a storm.

"Someone here should be able to fix this," he said to no one.

A young, fresh-faced girl in a candy striper uniform entered the room, a tidy stack of folded sheets between her hands. He grabbed her arm and pulled her over to the bedside. The sheets fell to the floor, and she gave a tiny yelp. Damon paid no mind.

"Why is she covered? She is not to be covered. Do you understand me? Do not cover her face, damn it."

"Mister, I-I—."

Damon's head dropped down at his vise-like grip on her arm, and his eyes widened. His hand opened, and he jerked it back as if scalded. Rubbing his forehead, then his eyes hard, he glanced around, as if seeing the room for the first time. He straightened, collecting himself enough to apologize.

"I — I'm so sorry. I just I'm sorry..."

The candy striper backed out of the room, nodding her head. But her eyes were huge as she reached behind her for the door frame. Once her fingertips found the metal frame she turned and rushed out, never to return to the room.

A short while later, a doctor in a lab coat strode in, then stopped short. Damon was tucking the sheet over my shoulders and smoothing my sea-damp hair from my face. He cleared his throat.

"Sir? I am Dr. Obowi. I performed...the assessment on your wife. Do you need any help making... arrangements?"

"I — no, they... her parents. Her parents are coming. We'll bring her home together. Thank you, Doctor."

"Perhaps you would like to wait out in the..."

"Thank you, no. I'll be staying with my wife."

Dr. Obowi opened his mouth, glanced from the bed to Damon, and closed it again. He tapped his clipboard a few times with the tip of his pen, then gave a curt nod.

"I'll see about getting you a change of closes, son. No need for you to catch pneumonia."

Moments later a nurse brought him a pair of sea-green foam scrubs and all but ordered him to put them on. She brought him a blanket, as well. Though she had a stern, all business face, she patted his shoulder before leaving him.

I smiled, grateful to the woman for her kindness toward Damon. He managed a quick nod. No one disturbed him, *us*, after that. The world went on around us. The skinny red hand on the clock ticked the seconds. The sun began to set. Noises came through the thin walls, beeps and blips, intercom announcements. Gurney wheels on the floor. And in one small, white-walled room with fluorescent lights above and tiled floor below, sat Damon on a green cushioned metal chair. Before him, his wife of four years, eleven months, and thirty days. At midnight, he glanced up at the clock above the door, then back to my form on the bed.

"Happy Anniversary, my love," he whispered.

FIVE
HEMINGWAY & AUSTEN

"The Very first moment I beheld him, my heart was irrevocably gone."
—Jane Austen, Love and Friendship

Damon and I met on May 31st, 2012. We married exactly one year later. Had one of us dared the other, I bet we'd have done it the very first day. Walk right out of the bookstore and straight into the town hall. I know *I* would have; I was that immediately in love, even if I didn't feel the same kind of certainty he did. *'Sometimes you just know.'* That's what Damon said. He was certain enough for both of us, and that was good enough for me. Honestly? I figured, *this guy is probably going to break my heart*, but I'd already decided he'd be so worth it. Fuck consequence.

But he'd fallen just as hard, just as equally. I found it mind-blowing. I'm not saying I think I'm unlovable or unworthy of such an obviously amazing guy. My self-confidence and self-worth quotient is satisfactory. Remember, I'm the girl who still believed there was a prince out there for her, after all. It's just...well, it's like any dream that comes true, you have to pinch yourself to trust it's really happening.

Damon, I discovered, was living my dream life— a freelance writer traveling the country. He had a story for every state, each more incredible than the last. The way he described the Havasu Falls in the Grand Canyon, the Longs Peak in the Rocky Mountains and the Garden of One Thousand Buddhas in Montana left me awestruck and speechless. He inhaled the world with the same reverence and love as he did that Hemingway book. Damon made me want to breathe his air and see through his eyes and live in his world. So, I guess we were both certain in our own ways. He was certain we were going to be together, I was certain I *wanted* us to be together.

When we left the bookstore that fateful night, the streetlights were lit, and stores all closed. Damon walked me to my car. It was a little white Corolla that would eventually take us through nearly all fifty states and almost home again before it died with a sad little sigh on the side of the road in Senoia, Georgia.

I slipped my hand in his as if it were the most natural thing in the world, and he swung our arms to the beat of our steps. There was a lilac bush, heavy with new blooms, next to the driver's side. I'd parked there purposely, intending to pick some to bring home.

Damon released my hand and held up a finger, then jogged around the car to the bush. After a few minutes, he returned with a handful of blooms.

"For you. Beauty for beauty."

He pressed them into my arms, save one dainty stem with a perfect cluster of purple blossoms. Damon brought this one to his nose, closed his eyes, and breathed in its heady scent. Then he held it under mine. A mischievous smile danced across his face as he spun the stem between his thumb and finger. It tapped against the tip of my nose. When I twitched my head back, he chuckled. Stepping in closer, he ran the flower across my cheek and tucked it behind my ear. And then, of course, he kissed me.

You know that perfect kiss, the one you sigh at when you see it in a movie? The one where the guy slips his fingers through the girls' hair and cups the back of her head, runs his thumb against her cheek and stares soulfully into her eyes just before they fall into the kiss of all time? Yeah, it was that and more. So much more.

Everyone falls in love with Damon when they meet him, just in different ways. Men love him because he's a man's man; he can drink a beer and change a tire, watch football, and talk politics. Small children loved him because he'll get on the floor and lumber around like a bear for them. Older children love him because he listens to them and he *sees* them, not through them like most adults. And women? Please. If you must wonder at all, then I've done a terrible job describing him. The only thing that matches Damon's outer beauty is his inner beauty. I've never met or seen any other man who'd I'd call beautiful (besides Cary Grant, my original standard by which all would be measured). He is *extraordinary*.

At the beginning of us, before I let myself trust him fully, I would get jealous and surly when women would fawn over him with their blatant doe eyes and fluttering hearts. Eventually, though, I learned to chill. Mostly. It was all credit to how Damon handled the attention.

'Thank you, very kind.' Or, *'This is my girlfriend. We're pleased to meet you.'*

Or some variation. He never gave room for flirtation, never gave the wrong impression. Once, a casual acquaintance of mine— an especially attractive acquaintance— saw him at a bar. He'd been waiting for me, but I was running behind and ultimately had to cancel. A week or so later, I ran into her at the coffee shop.

"So," she said with a smirk and an arched eyebrow, "I met your boyfriend the other night."

"Oh? How did you know he was my boyfriend?"

She laughed and shook her head, abashed.

"Well, I kinda, sorta, totally hit on him."

It was my turn to raise an eyebrow. My spine stiffened, and I gripped my cup tighter in anticipation of what was to come.

"Whoa, whoa, relax. He shot me down. Unequivocally, too. And so politely! I, uh, was pretty impressed, so I said, *'well, she's one lucky girl.'* You know what he said?"

I didn't, but I had an idea.

"He said, '*no, I'm the lucky one, by far.*' Then he went on for another twenty minutes giving a dissertation of all things 'Birdie.' Obviously, that's not a common name, so I said, '*wait, Birdie Taylor Thomas?*' and he was like, '*why yes!*' so I'm like, '*um, we totally went to school together!*' Anyhow, I know more about you now than I did from four years of Spanish together. Congrats, you've got yourself a keeper, sweetie."

She clinked her coffee cup against mine in salute. We chatted for a bit longer, then went our separate ways, her with a slightly bruised ego, me with my heart bursting. Sorry, girls, but my man has eyes just for me.

Only, now I'm gone.

SIX
HOME BY THE SEA

How you've turned my world, you precious thing.
Everything I've done, I've done for you.
I move the stars for no one.
    —Jareth, Labyrinth

"Hey, man, it's good to see you getting out of the house. How, uh, how you holdin' up?"

Charlie, one of his writer friends from way back, has come to call on his bereaved pal. I've always liked Charlie. He is a huge man, with hands the size of oven mitts, and a voice so deep it rumbled in your chest when he spoke. He could lift a car with those hands. But I've also seen him rescue a frantic butterfly at my kitchen window, in those massive hands. He coaxed and cupped it, murmuring *'you're alright, little guy. I've got you,'* and carried it to safety without crushing it. He is a gentle giant.

"Not sure if you can call thirty yards from the house 'getting out' but, yeah. Birdie...she, uh, she loved it out here the best."

It's true, I did. *Do*. We'd spent more than we could afford on the beach house. But the moment I stepped out onto the balcony and saw the ocean waves rolling against the beach mere yards away, I was enamored. All Damon had to see was that look in my eyes. The sun was setting over the water, the orange-red light danced and sparkled like jewels. The beauty of that view had moved me to tears. Or maybe it was the thought of spending the rest of our lives amidst such breathtaking beauty.

Whatever it was, he resolved to make it happen for me. Perhaps this is bragging. I apologize if it sounds so, but I'm not exaggerating when I tell you— he would move a mountain with his bare hands for me if he thought it would bring me joy. To be loved like that… well, it's incomparable to anything else.

The agent— a woman with perfect salon-styled and frosted blonde hair, shrewd cornflower-blue eyes, and red lipstick— had click-clacked in on her black patent leather high heels right behind us. Everything about her was sharp, efficient and self-possessed. Dana Fontana, Real Estate Agent, signified her lapel pin. She pressed the edge of her clipboard against her pantsuit and listed the homes many features in her chirping, chipper saleswoman voice.

"As you can see, the bedroom balcony offers a spectacular view of…"

"We'll take it."

"…the ocean. P-pardon me?"

The real estate agent stammered. Damon had interrupted her recitation; she was caught off-guard and taken off script. My eyes went wide as I too stared at Damon, unsure if I should believe my ears. He nodded, that huge mischievous smile of his crinkling the corners of his eyes. He tossed me a wink and then turned to the agent.

"I said we'll take it. Full asking price. Start the paperwork, please."

Of course, nothing goes so easily, but by the fall, we were moving boxes and furniture into our beachfront bungalow. Damon had dubbed it 'Birdie's Nest.' A sign above the door and all. For four years, no matter where we went, we couldn't wait to get back home. It surprised me, this about Damon. I'd expected him to feel confined after having spent so much time as a traveling nomad, but it wasn't so.

"Birdie, we could be traveling the world, or living here, or in a city apartment, or a village hut for all I care. Doesn't matter one bit, so long as we're together."

"Hmmm, let's see if you'll say that after we run out of coffee the first time and I turn into Satan. Might change your mind, buddy."

"Ha! Fat chance. I tolerate your snoring, so…"

"Shut up! I do not snore!"

"You do, but it's adorable."

That was the closest we ever really got to arguing. Don't get me wrong; we've had plenty of *disagreements* and *differences of opinion*. God, we're not robots. We just didn't *fight*. Trust me when I say, Damon is your stereotypical guy. Won't ask for directions, leaves the toilet seat up, and never seems to recall where the garbage pail is. I'm your stereotypical woman. I constantly tell him where to go and how to get there, the *right* way to do things, and I change my mind as frequently as I blink. Well...*was. Told. Used to.*

Charlie is studying him, a flurry of quick side glances meant to be discrete. Even with his eyes trained on the horizon, Damon knows. This is what people do now, now he is a widower at thirty-nine. They stare when they think he's not looking. They keep their eye contact brief as if the death of a loved one was contagious and transmittable by looks. They start sentences, then stop. Sometimes they lay awkward arm or shoulder pats that linger too long.

In the first week, casseroles piled up in the freezer and fridge. No one knew what to say or how to help Damon, so the women bustled and fretted, speaking in gentle voices, using careful words. The men cracked beers and small innocuous jokes. They mentioned the weather or the Red Sox in sentences that trailed off at the ends. Damon, being Damon, wanted to help *them* help him, but he didn't have the energy.

"Jack still has his preseason tickets, we should, uh, go to some games. Like we — like usual. It'll be a good distraction for you."

"I appreciate that Charlie," his tone is sharp, "but I don't want to be *distracted*, okay? I'm good. I— I'm good right here."

Charlie nods and picks at the label on his beer bottle and then follows Damon's gaze across the ocean. The men are quiet for a time. The surf is loud. Damon takes a long pull from his bottle, goes to speak. No sound comes out. His chest rises, he scratches his neck and exhales through his mouth. He tries again.

"I mean it, thank you. You've— you and Jack, you guys have been amazing. I don't know how I'd have gotten through those first..." He falters, "Birdie, she, uh, she fricking loved you guys so damn much..."

The last word catches in his chest. The men drink their beers. Charlie scratches his eyebrow. What he's really doing is swiping at a tear with his broad palm. He struggles past a hard knot in his throat to find something else to say, something on another topic. Damon knows it, I'm sure, but says nothing.

In the end, they decide to say nothing. Charlie and Damon, with me in tow, walk back up the embankment. Quiet steps on sand covered boards lead us across the short boardwalk to Birdie's Nest. The men drink a case of beer with their pizza and talk about things neither will remember afterward. Charlie leaves the next morning, extracting a promise from Damon to come out and see him soon.

Maya and Abe, the neighbors across the street, make their way up the driveway as Charlie backs out. With a casserole, of course. Kale and quinoa with the oxymoron of meatless meat and vegan cheese. She emphasizes the *vegan* as if it held great importance. Damon keeps them at the door. Maya hedges forward and angles her head around Damon, into the foyer behind him. They are hoping for an invite inside.

We never socialized with the Harvicks when I was alive, although they seemed nice enough. If you like overzealous environmentalists, who drive hybrid cars with various activist bumper stickers on the back. Maya sold handmade jewelry from her stand in the farmer's market. Abe was a therapist who worked for free one day a week in the city, counseling at-risk youth. They drove their tiny car all around town and talked about recycling as if it were their religion.

We may or may not have made fun of them when I was alive. Fine, we did. Often. Okay, *I* made fun of the Harvicks, and Damon *tsk—tsk*'ed me as he laughed. No one is laughing now, though.

From under the bushiest eyebrows, I've ever seen, Abe's shrewd eyes take in Damon's appearance. His unkempt hair, his pizza stained white t-shirt, down to his baggy sweatpants and bare feet.

"So, Damon. How are you in your process?"

Damon slow blinks at Abe for a moment.

"My...process?"

"Your *process*, Damon. Your grief stages, you must be aware of your stages, friend. Critical for healing."

"Abe— let the man be!"

Maya purses her thin lips in annoyance. She not-so-gently swats Abe in his paunchy, middle-aged stomach. He makes a little sound like '*uhf,*' and it cracks me up. I look at Damon to see if he's got that telltale chin quiver of barely restrained laughter, but there's nothing on his face but... nothing.

Maya turns her close-set, olive green eyes to Damon, assessing him from head to toe as Abe had done. *Her* look calls to mind a hungry lioness looking for lunch. A scrawny, starving, lioness. Good luck with that, Maya dear. You're not Damon's type. He doesn't like thin-lipped hairy-legged women, thank you very much. This would be a great time for one of those ghost superpowers. Trust me, Maya Harvick would be wearing her stupid kale casserole by now if I could figure out how to make that happen. Hmm, I guess my jealous streak never really went away. Whatever.

"Well," Damon breaks the awkward lull, startling everyone. "Thank you for coming by. And for the...casserole. But I — uh, I've got to get back to work, so uh, thanks again."

As the door closes, Maya's voice squeaks through the crack:

"The tray is recyclable!"

Damon locks the door for good measure and leans against it. Looking down at the cloth covered dish, he gives a derisive snort.

"Fuck, Birdie. You would've loved that."

He'd begun doing this — talking to the air...*to me*— about a week ago. The first time he did it, I jumped for joy. Literally. I believed for a moment he saw me, standing in my favorite spot in the house. Our balcony overlooking the ocean. But he was talking *through* me, to the sea and the air.

"Oh, Birdie," he had sighed, bowing his head.

"Damon! I'm here, I'm right *here*, babe."

But when he didn't react to the sound of my voice, I understood. Grandpa Mack had done this after Grandma Grace died. He always included her in conversations. *'Our girl Taylor is growing so fast, isn't she Gracie?'.* He kept a place set for her at the table until the day he died, six years after her. I thought it was beautiful and sweet, and so sad.

I think the same now, as I watch *my* beautiful, sweet, sad husband try to keep his dead wife's presence alive. But I also think, *no, this won't do.* Grandpa Mack was eighty—three. Damon is thirty—nine, he can't spend the rest of his life talking to a dead woman. For now, though... well, I know I'm selfish, but I get to pretend along with him.

"Birdie, *why*? Why did this happen to us? To you?"

"Aw, babe. I don't know."

"I'm so sorry I made you do that damn jump. You were scared. You died scared and *alone*."

"No, honey, no. I'm okay. There was a boy..."

"I will hate myself forever, Birdie."

"Oh, babe, stop, please. Don't..."

Damon turned away from the balcony and strode back inside. He closed the door between us. My heart sank at the loud click, the door separating us like that, but something tugged at my mind.

The boy.

SEVEN
WHISPERS

Callin' out her name I'm dreamin'
Reflections of a face I'm seein'
It's her voice that keeps on haunting me
Send Her My Love, Journey

Damon didn't see the boy, the handsome child with amber eyes. Why? This means something; I *know* it does. Going through the mental arsenal of every book, movie, and made-for-television show I've ever seen on the subject tells me the obvious. The boy is an angel. *Of course*, he is. I think back to what he said.

"Don't be scared, lady. I've done it a bunch of times" and then *"It's okay, lots of people are scared. It's your time, though."*

It takes on new meaning now. I dissect the sentences.

"I've done it a bunch of times."

What does that mean? Has he died a bunch of times? Or he's helped *others* die a bunch of times?

Or just that he's cliff dived a bunch of times? Then, how can I forget his last sentence?

"*It's your time, though.*"

No need to wonder what *that* meant, not anymore. Once again, I find myself pacing. I want, no, I need answers. I need to find the boy.

My gaze returns to Damon, leaned against the door, staring blindly at the stupid casserole. I can't bear the thought of leaving him. Assuming that's even an option.

This is the only place I want to be. Near Damon, where I can still see his face and smell his clean scent. I think this, and then realize we are each other's ghost. Each is behind a one—way mirror. Invisible, but *there*. I followed him around like a shadow for a time. Like a puppy, hopeful and eager for attention.

From across the kitchen, I watch him throw Abe and Maya Harvick's kale casserole in the trash.

"Fuck recycling," he mutters and stomps upstairs. In a moment, I hear the squeal of the shower faucets turning.

Of all the things I *haven't* learned yet about the afterlife, the one thing I'm discovering is the irregularity of time. Time is, well, it's weird when you're dead. I mean, it's weird when you're alive, too. But when you're *alive*, it travels in a pretty linear way as far as we can tell. Our clock goes in an exact cycle, from twelve a.m. to twelve p.m. Round and round it goes. Each second, minute and hour goes neatly and orderly marching along. It doesn't become three o'clock after five o'clock, nor does it skip from six o'clock to ten. Sure, it may *feel* like it sometimes, but we know it doesn't. Here in dead world — at least my version of it — time is bouncy.

It jumps from one 'now' to the next. This moment it is Sunday, *blink*, and suddenly it's Tuesday or Thursday. It's jarring and unsettling, but what choice do I have but to get used to it? Oh, if I could *control* it, though. Now that would be nice. I have a suspicion I'm being led around, that there are some rhyme and reason to the bounces. But I'll be damned if I can figure it out yet.

I've lost days and weeks in my post-death state. As a result, I'm learning how to accept every moment we're given. Something I was never good at when I was alive, I'm afraid. Death has taught me to be present. How ironic.

Right now, the powers-that-be have let me join Damon in the steam filled bathroom. I sit on the sink counter, and lean back against the long mirror, and watch Damon's naked form through the blooms of steam that fog the shower door. He's letting the water rain over his bowed head; his fists are against the tiles. Intermittent sounds—sniffs, I realize, are coming from behind the shower door. Instinct forces me from the counter to the shower door. I press both my hand and my head against the warm glass. He is crying.

His tears mix with the water and disappear in the drain. There's something hot and wet on my cheek; I wipe my salty tears away with my fingertips. It is the first time I've cried since I died. I'm crying for him, for me. For *us*. Our future, or what it was supposed to be.

Damon pounds his fist against the tile, hard enough to rattle the glass door and topple the conditioner. *My* conditioner, the one that smells like honey and clementine. I jump back, retreat to the sink again. I know exactly how he feels right now. Angry. Robbed.

Abruptly, Damon shuts the water off and opens the shower door. He's forgotten his towel on the counter, as he always does, and walks naked and dripping across the bathroom. He is standing right in front of me, exposed, vulnerable. Beautiful. And because I can, because when I was alive, I could, I run my hands over his shoulders, letting my fingertips dance along his clavicle, down his strong arms, his hands. They twitch, closing around mine for the briefest of seconds. His long lashes flutter against his damp cheeks; his breath is slow, unsteady. Carefully, I slip off the counter and stand before him. I rake my nails against his thighs. Goosebumps rise on his skin, he is growing hard against me. His pulse beats in his throat, I press my lips against it. He can *feel* me, I know it. I will him not to think, just allow the senses to rule. It's working. But then, I ruin it.

"Damon."

It's a whisper, involuntary at that, but his eyes jerk open and his body tenses. He looks around the bathroom, confused. His erection subsides, and he grabs his towel, drying off roughly. Using the side of his palm, he wipes the steam from the mirror and shakes his head at his reflection. Then, with a look of self-loathing, he pushes back the long hair off his forehead.

"Pull yourself together, man. Birdie's gone."

"I'm here, babe."

He turns away and exits the room. My hand is still outstretched, poised to feel. And then it's eight days later.

EIGHT
OLD FRIENDS
Et tu, Brute?
—William Shakespeare, Julius Caesar

Summer in a beach town, it's a resident's hell. Especially in July. Navigating through the narrow streets becomes a challenge. Sweaty families sloth across the road lugging chairs, umbrellas, bags, and coolers. Their sunscreen streaked children whine for ice cream. Teenage wannabe—surfer boys lug their Wal—Mart boards to the shore. All the while, they check to see if the teenage bikini-clad girls are following them. In turn, the girls with their burgeoning sexuality and fragile self—confidence, giggle and put on airs for them.

Damon dodges and brakes and maneuvers around them like a pro. He has always gotten a kick out of it all; making a game out of avoiding them, even. It was easy, he claimed. Vacationers always traveled in time waves. When they sunbathed, when they hit the stores, the movies. All predictable. So, he plans all *our* things around them. We stroll down to the beach at three o'clock, walk or drive to the stores at seven. Movies, not at all. I was never so gracious as he was. I couldn't stand their blatant disrespect for the beach and the ocean. Or the pushy way they took over the grocery store aisles and bought up all my favorite wine.

"Now, Birdie," Damon would scold, "we don't own the beach, we have to share it with everyone."

"It's a private beach. There are rules."

"*Yes*, and most of our neighbors are seasonal, they rent the properties out. We knew this when we bought the house, my love. I have a solution, you know."

"Oh? What's that? Get rid of them with a flesh-eating bacterium scare?"

"Wow. No, Birdie, I was thinking more like— wait for it... a vacation!"

"Really? To where?"

"Well, what's your second favorite place in the world?"

"Um, Melissa and Doug's farm, duh!"

"Exactly. They invited us up for a couple of weeks. What do you say?"

"Oh, my God! Yes! *Thank* you, babe. When do we leave? Now? Can we leave right now?"

Stealthily, like a ninja, Damon had already packed our bags. We left the next day for New Hampshire. It became our annual trip, up until last year. This year would've marked our fifth trip, but it wasn't my death that ended these yearly treks. It was something I'd not been able to tell Damon about, and now I never can. Our last visit...

...

Doug bellowed from the front porch, three beer bottles in his hands.

"It's about time you two got here! Jake and Nicky have been driving me crazy."

When Damon and I walked up, he loud-whispered,

"So's Mel, but don't tell her I said that."

Melissa had snuck up behind him in the doorway.

"Busted, Doug. I hear *every*thing, buddy. Don't listen to him, guys. Come on in. How was your trip?"

Before we could answer, Damon's' ankles were tackled by two rowdy, towheaded little boys with shouts of *'Uncle Damon's here!'* Mel and I left the boys to their roughhousing, and we went to the quiet of the kitchen.

"I swear, those three are worse than the goats."

"You should switch 'em out— bring the goats in the house and send the boys to the barn."

"They'd be a lot neater, that's for sure."

We laughed and chatted companionly as we loaded up the cutting boards with cheeses and prosciutto, grapes and figs, roasted vegetables and honeyed garlic. It was like being at one of those farm-to-table restaurants that were cropping up everywhere. Only better.

I'd always marveled at how easily Mel and I became friends. Truly a testament to her friendliness and *not* mine. I'd always been a bit of a loner; content to be in my own little world writing my Austen-esque stories and living in my fantasy world. A classic introvert, I kept my distance from people whenever possible. But with Mel, it was different.

The first time we met was right there, at their farm. Doug, towering in the doorway, beer in hand, had greeted us with a brash bellow.

"Welcome to Miller's Farm, where the beer is cold, and the ladies are hot!"

He had slapped his knee and gave a bemused laugh at his own joke. I remember glancing at Damon, my eyebrows raised. He shrugged and gave a half-hearted apology.

"Sorry, babe," he stage-whispered, "shoulda prepared you better for ole Doug. He's a character. Harmless, though."

After Damon had introduced me, Doug explained we may not see Mel for a while.

"One of her goats is in a *'difficult labor,'*" he rolled his eyes and put air quotes around the words, "and she can't leave the barn until she knows mother and kid are alright."

"Oh, wow. I've never seen a goat being born. Can I join her, you think?"

Doug shrugged and said, "Suit yourself, sweetheart. Personally, I'm staying the hell away. Goats are *her* territory, not mine, thank you very much."

"There's my sensitive, compassionate friend I know and love."

Damon laughed, clapping his old friend on the back.

I left them to their manly men speak and crossed the yard to the weathered brown barn. Inside I found Mel and her goats. Baggy faded overalls covered a huge baby bump, and her long brown hair was in loose braids. A pair of hooves protruded grotesquely from the back end of a tan and white goat. They were grasped in Mel's hands. She didn't act at all surprised to see me, just smiled and said,

"Ha, I *knew* you'd come out to help me. Doug guessed you'd stay by Damon's side. He owes me a week of dish duty, thanks!"

"You're welcome. What can I do?"

"Grab me that towel over there. This one is breech, so I'm helping it out."

"Literally. Wow. Is it — will it be okay?"

"Ah, sure. It's fairly common with goats. You're exactly as Damon described you — well, once I translated it to regular mortal speak."

"Oh, boy. Knowing Damon, I can only imagine what he said!"

It's true, Damon can't say things like *'she has long blonde hair and hazel eyes and is five foot—three inches.'* No, Damon will have told Mel...

"She has hair like the sands of the Sahara in sunlight. Her eyes are like Autumn splendor, she is diminutive but mighty."

Mel recited Damon's words back to me with a laugh, all while still extracting a kid from its mother's rear with slow care. Through my own laughter, I recited what Damon had said about her.

"Mel is the epitome of Mother Earth, all grace, and strength and boundless love for all things great and small. Her smile is wide, her hair is wild. She is Gaea, Goddess of Earth."

"Oh, my *God*. He's been calling me Gaea, Goddess of Earth so long, I'm starting to believe him. As you can see by all this."

She let one hand off the hooves for a moment to wave an arm around to encompass the farm before giving one last gentle tug, then the kid was out. It was slimy, limp, and silent. I thought it was dead.

"Towel, please. Thanks. Step back, you might not want to get this stuff on your pretty dress."

I did as she said, and Mel carefully swung the baby goat from side to side. Discharge came out of its mouth and nose, and to be honest — I gagged a little at the sight. Suddenly the kid began to buck and bleat, and she set it down on the ground by its mother. I was awestruck.

"There! Alright, Sahara Hair, you hungry?"

"Well, Gaea, I could sure use a drink."

Mel patted her very pregnant belly with both hands and laughed the deep, hearty laugh that pregnant women get in their late stages.

"Have one for me too, will ya?"

We walked back to the house, each of us carrying a bucket for scraps. The men were on the porch in rocking chairs drinking their beers. Mel waddled the way very pregnant women tend to do, but she still did *everything* while we were there. It was apparent right from the start.

Mel pulled the dishes down from the cabinet and replenished the drinks. Doug nodded but kept talking. She fed the dogs, took the trash out back, answered phone calls, and then brought the dogs back in. Doug? Raised his empty beer once, gave it a little shake and nodded his head. When she saw my stare, she rolled her eyes in a way that said, '*Oh, this guy.*'

Don't get me wrong, I love doing things for Damon. *Loved* to. I'm not one of those militant feminists who think it's a horror to serve a man. But if Damon didn't appreciate everything—and I mean everything—the way he does, I'd have no problem telling him to get his own damn beer. I can't fathom this kind of ungrateful, unreciprocated servitude.

How to describe Doug? Hmm. *I'd* describe Doug as the kind of guy whose smile dropped the moment your back turned. If I were to channel *Damon's* literary proclivity, perhaps I'd say something more, like, '*Doug is a man of impressive, even commanding height. His sandy hair recedes from his forehead as if both sides of his widow's peak were racing against each other. His eyes are the color of slate, his shark-like smile rarely reaches them.*'

But, I don't believe Damon saw this about his friend. He's blinded by the memories of the friendship from their younger days. But then, to the casual observer, Doug is all amiable hospitality, at least, on the surface he is.

His friendliness is *too* friendly. His agreeability is *overly* amiable. His laughter is a kind of bellowing, complete with back claps and knee slaps. And then there was his smile—the one that never reached his eyes. He struck me as a B-list actor playing a role. Husband, host, and father-to-be. But when the cameras stopped filming, and the curtain fell, he was something different. Very different.

The only thing I thought was genuine with Doug, was his admiration of Damon. It bordered on idolization, really. It was plain in his every action, every conversation, right from the first meeting.

On that day, when Mel and I had left the barn, and joined the guys on the porch, Doug had started right away.

"Damon, man, did you tell Birdie about the time you climbed Mt. Haleakala? Crazy, just crazy! You know how to *live*, man."

"I did indeed. In fact, we're going on a trip to Hawaii next month, and we're going to do the hike together."

Damon raised the amber beer bottle up to his lips, then paused, bottle hovering, and looking at me as he added,

"Funny to hear someone else call you Birdie."

"Oh," exclaimed Doug, his face going pink, "did I say Birdie? My bad — I meant to say, Taylor. Don't wanna steal your *term of endearment*, or anything!"

"Or my girl, hopefully."

Damon winked to show he was teasing. Perhaps I imagined it, but I recall sensing an awkward pause hovering in the kitchen. Mel was quick to fill it.

"If you two don't stop talking about days gone past, *I'm* going to steal her away from both of you. As a matter of fact, let's you and I go in and get some wine. I think I'll have a small glass after all."

In the kitchen, I had to ask her something that had nagged at me since the barn.

"So, why'd Doug think I'd have stayed by Damon side, and not gone to meet you?"

"I— oh. Well, he just..."

"I just went by history, sweetheart! All of Damon's' girls have glued themselves to his side. I have— *had*, I mean— to pry 'em off with a crowbar! Isn't that right, Mel?"

Doug had snuck into the kitchen behind us, startling us.

"*Doug*," Mel admonished, her eyes slanting as she tipped her head to the side.

"What? I'm speaking the truth. Bir — *Taylor* here is a big girl, she knows guys like Damon have a long line of broken hearts behind them. Right sweetheart?"

Before I could stammer an answer, Damon was there, behind me, his hair tickling my ear as he pressed his lips to my shoulder. He spoke against my skin.

"Don't listen to that barbarian's tall tales."

We all laughed, the awkward moment diffused like mist. But Doug wasn't ready to drop it.

"Oh, come now, my friend. Don't be modest! Sweetheart, this guy... why even Mel had a bit of a thing for Damon once upon a time. Didn't you, Mel?"

Mel flushed and shot an apologetic look my way, then another warning glare at Doug.

"Douglas, you know perfectly well *that* is not true. Taylor, don't even listen to him. The real story — and he knows this — is Damon had one particularly aggressive hanger-on. What was her name again, Damon?"

"Rita. No, Reba."

"Right — Reba. God, she was crazy. Anyhow, we're at one of those cliché college frat parties…"

"Before he dropped out and left us behind for a life of action and adventure," interrupted Doug.

"…and across the room I see *this* guy," she continued and wagged a thumb in Damon's direction, "looking all traumatized and uncomfortable as crazy—drunk Rita—Reba tries to dry hump him."

I nearly spit my wine out. Through her own laughter, Mel continued.

"Anyhow, we make eye contact, and he looked so helpless with those big brown puppy eyes of his, and I took pity on your poor guy here…"

"As I recall, you were pointing and laughing at me…" Damon interjected.

"…and rescued him by pretending to be his girlfriend. His very slutty, touchy-feely girlfriend. Scared her away."

Mel turned her gaze, now softer, almost wistful, to Doug, whose expression was unreadable.

"When *this* big lug walked over, that was it for me. Head over heels, pathetically in love."

"Hmm, well that's her story, and she's stuck to it all these years…"

Doug appeared to give it deep consideration.

"So, I guess I'll buy it. What do you say, sweetheart? You buy their story?"

I glanced from Damon to Mel, and back to Damon again, tapping a finger to my chin and squinting my eyes at them. I smirked, and Damon grinned back, beer bottle hovering before his lips again, waiting.

"Yes. Consider it bought."

I winked at Damon and clinked wine glasses with Mel, and the rest of the visit went by without further reference.

I never told Damon about my first impression of Doug. Or that it lasted throughout our friendship with him and Melissa. Maybe I should have, and what happened *last* summer never would've. I like to say it was because I didn't want to hurt Damon or jeopardize a valued friendship. It's true, of course. But, if I'm to be truthful, I was selfish. *Am* selfish. I wanted our movie perfect foursome, the Harrison's at the Millers. I wanted the illusion.

I'm stalling once again. Cowardly, I know. Very well. There's no gentle way to say it. The last night, on the last ever visit to Miller's Farm, Douglas Miller tried to rape me. I wish I could believe he was drunk, or he was confused, or… I don't know, whatever else you say to convince yourself something bad didn't happen. But he wasn't —at least no moreso than usual — and it did happen.

It was around two a.m. The postcard-perfect farmhouse was silent but for the usual sighs and ticks of an old house. We were in the guest room at the far end of the upstairs hall. The one that smells of lavender and chamomile. Damon was in a deep sleep, his eyes fluttering behind their lids, his lips parted. He was peaceful in his repose. I was not.

I'd had one of my recurring nightmares. My drowning one this time. I've had them for as long as I can remember, and there's no good explanation for them. I'm an excellent swimmer (if I say so myself) and I've never had a traumatic experience in or around water, ever. Unless you count that whole thing where I died. Not the waters fault, though. The blame rests on my bum heart.

If I'm to believe dream interpretations, then drowning dreams depict a *'fear of being overwhelmed by difficult emotions or anxieties.'* It makes sense. I *was* always an anxious kid and, as Damon can attest, expressing my emotions has always been a challenge for me.

In this nightmare, the sky is always red. I find myself beside a cement pond full of bizarre and terrifying fish-like creatures. They're so clear, so *vivid*, with wide, mad eyes and angry, teeth-filled mouths. Despite my revulsion, I lean closer to see them. I lose my balance and slide down the steep embankment. I am submerged in dense, gelatin-like water. My movements are sluggish, I'm disoriented. There are menacing snakes of all different colors weaving towards me. I've managed to grab a weak, wobbly stick, and I'm pushing them away as best I can. The stick bends and threatens to snap at any moment. My chest is getting tight, and panic is taking over. I know I'm about to gasp for air, but just before I swallow a mouthful of snakes and water, I awaken with a shuddering gasp. It is always this way. Was, I mean.

Slick sweat coated my neck, and my heart pounded with a sickening violence. Damon slept beside me, one bare leg, pale in the moonlight, thrown over my waist. I slipped out from underneath him, wiped the sweat from my brow, and willed my breath to slow. I was wide awake, the dream still vivid behind my eyes. If I went downstairs, I'd risk waking the others, If I stayed in bed, I'd go stir crazy. *The barn.* I could spend some time with the goats and Dante, Melissa's new donkey.

There was a balcony off the bedroom with stairs that led out to the yard, facing the barn. I glanced over at my shorts hanging over the floral print armchair. Damon's t-shirt brushed against my thighs. It covered my ass well enough. It's not like a bunch of goats, and a donkey was going to judge me, anyhow. So, I grabbed my boots and tiptoed out the balcony door, down the damp dew stairs. I pulled my boots on at the bottom step and ran across the wet grass, leaving behind a trail of prints. I was already grinning at the thought of Dante's big black nose nuzzling carrots from my hand.

Inside the barn it was dark and sweet smelling, the stalls had been turned and the hay fresh. As soon as I rolled opened the wide door, I could hear Dante snicker and chuff in anticipation of a visitor. I skip—ran to his stall. A voice in the dimness made me jump.

"So, you found me, huh?"

"Jesus! Doug, you scared the shit out of me. I - I didn't know anyone else was up."

He came out of the shadow, a cigarette between his fingers. He'd told Mel he'd quit. A lie.

"Oh, sorry. Thought you were Mel, hunting me down. Don't tell her about this, huh?"

He waved the cigarette, now between his thumb and fingers. Then he flicked it into in a bucket of water intended for the goats to drink from. It gave a short hiss.

"Can't sleep on hot nights like this, even with the A.C. on. Same for you?"

He sauntered toward me, his eyes like slits. I remember it now as predatorily, but did I see it then? Yes, but not until it was too late.

"No, I had — yeah, I couldn't sleep."

Talk about my nightmares with Doug? No, that's just too...*intimate*, especially at two in the morning, as I stood half naked in a barn with my husband's best friend. The cool barn air raised goosebumps on my half—bare ass. I was more conscious than ever of my lack of clothing. But the mind is a funny thing, isn't it? Even when every sense tells you one thing, you insist on believing another. At this moment, I wanted to believe I was silly. Ridiculous, even. So, I shook my head, more at myself than anything.

This is Doug, *for Christ's sake! Stop acting weird. Act normal, damn it.*

Instead of leaving the barn and returning to the warm comfort of Damon and our cozy bed, I gave him a shaky smile, tucked my hair behind my ear, and dug for a carrot from the basket by Dante's stall. The whole time, I was careful to not expose my underpants.

Act normal. Act normal. Act normal.

Immediately, Dante approached the gate, chuffing and twitching his downy soft, black-tipped ears and nibbled the outstretched carrot. He tried to pull it out of my grasp, but I murmured placating words and chuckled at him. Feigning nonchalance and failing, I was sure.

Doug said nothing, but I was certain his eyes were boring holes in my back, or more likely, my ass. I kept one hand on the hem of my shirt, conscious of its length — or lack of.

"Don't hold it on my account."

"What? Doug!" My voice, I could hear it was an octave too high. "You're too much."

I laughed a forced sound. It was one thing when he made off-color jokes and comments in front of Damon. Then we could all laugh and say, *'Oh, Doug!'* And no one took him seriously. But when you're alone in the near dark, with hardly any clothes on, well… it becomes very different. It was enough for me to finally take it as my cue to leave, so I let the carrot fall to the ground and wiped my hands on my shirt. I started to say,

"Well, guess I'll head on back up…"

I turned around to face him, the beginning of *'goodnight'* on my lips. Before I could speak, Doug was on me. It happened so damn fast. He slammed me hard against the gate rails of Dante's stall and grabbed my wrists. One of his long, thick legs worked to get between my bare legs.

This isn't happening.

He had boxers on, and the coarse, wiry hair on his leg was like sandpaper on my skin. I instinctively turned my head down, away from his, as he tried to kiss me. *He's trying to* kiss *me*, my mind dumbly registered. His stubble scraped hard against the corner my mouth, I cried out. It all happened so fast. *He* was so fast, damn it.

"Doug, *stop*! Stop it, damn it!"

"No one's here, Birdie, you don't have to fight it. On second thought, keep it up. I like it."

He was panting against my neck, his breath stank of cigarette. His beard stubble pierced minuscule holes in my throat, as he tried to maneuver between my legs. I felt *it* against my thigh, he was rock hard. He was so fucking strong.

My God, he is going to rape me. No, I'm misunderstanding this.

The smell of cigarette and his aftershave filled my nostrils as I struggled against him. I was almost free until he grabbed a fistful of my hair. He yanked my head back hard against the rails of Dante's gate. I yelped, and tears of pain stung my eyes. I couldn't move an inch without fear of my hair tearing from my scalp. Without even looking, I knew he was freeing his erection from his boxers. He hissed into my ear:

"You want this, admit…"

He is going to rape me.

I went still. Doug was too strong, if I stopped fighting, it would be over faster. I turned my eyes away and stared up into the rafters and waited for the violation. His free hand was at the front of my underwear, his fingers against my pubic hair. But just as he began to yank the thin material down, he jumped back with a loud cry, jerking his hand —the one with a fistful of my hair — to his chest. I slumped from the sudden release, the bones in my legs like rubber, unable to support me at first. Only part of me understood what I was seeing, but it was enough to mobilize me.

Dante had bitten him, hard. Blood welled on his knuckles, then seeped through his fingers. We both stared in shock as it dripped to the dirt floor. His deflated cock hung limply through the opening of his boxers. My stomach lurched, and my throat constricted. I swallowed hard against the rising sickness and pulled myself up, using the edge of Dante's stall for support.

My scalp burned, and my heart pounded in my throat as my eyes darted around the barn. *I need a weapon.* There was a pitchfork propped against a stall door. It glinted in the moonlight, beckoning me. An image of me charging him, stabbing the sharp steel prongs to his throat, sprang to mind. Emboldened by that image, the spark of outrage lit in my gut. I gritted my teeth hard, and narrowed my eyes at him, tensing for another attack. But Doug was still staring at his blood-soaked hand. I for the moment was forgotten. The part of my brain that still had a shred of logic hissed a command.

Get out of here, now. Get to Damon.

Damon. Yes, Damon will… fix this. A strange phrase, I know. But when something is broken, you want the person you trust most to fix it. But what I really meant? What I really wanted Damon to do? I wanted Damon to come out and kill him. Another voice in my head. *This will* devastate *Damon. Think of Damon.* He *will* kill him.

The image of him in handcuffs was a splash of icy cold water, clearing my mind. These rapid-fire thoughts, all as my breath wheezed and hissed in and out, my heart thundered. Seconds. So many thoughts in just seconds. The decision made, I backed away.

I sidestepped Doug and backed out of the barn, not taking my eyes off him as he stared down at his hand. When I was sure he wasn't following me, I did run. Across the yard, to the balcony stairs.

Do you know, I still stopped to take my boots off? Even then, it struck me funny. I'd been almost raped by my husband's best friend (*how cliché*, I had the wit to think) but I took my boots off so as not to wake my sleeping husband. A crazy sounding barking laugh burst from my lips. I stifled it, shocked. I was *in* shock, of course.

I couldn't go inside, not yet. So, I curled up in a tight ball in the corner of the balcony beside the fake potted fern, afraid the Doug would see me up there otherwise, and I rocked. The moonlight turned everything strange shades of gray.

I won't cry, damn it.

I said that to myself over and over, a hundred times, maybe more. This is what shock is like, I suppose. When I could finally stand again, I tiptoed inside. Damon was as I'd left him. Though desperate for a shower, I feared waking him. So, instead, I snuck into the connected bathroom and turned the hot water faucet on low. When it became as hot as I could stand, I soaked a washcloth and lathered Mel's lavender soap into the fibers. Then I scrubbed every part of my body that bastard had touched. With my skin on fire, I climbed back into bed, careful to not disturb my husband. I listened for sounds of Doug all night, terrified he was outside our door, or at the balcony entry. Waiting for me.

At some point, I did manage to fall asleep, because the next thing I opened my eyes to, was weak daylight streaming in through the windows and birds singing. I feigned a headache and asked Damon to bring my coffee upstairs and give my apologies.

"Of course, babe. Hey, what happened there?"

He pointed to the corner of his own mouth and jutted his chin at me. When I stared at him blankly, he leaned on the bed and cupped my chin in his hand, turning my face to get a better look. My stomach dropped.

"I — I must've scratched myself in my sleep. No worries."

"Poor love. Did you have another dream? I wish you'd wake me when that happens, I feel awful sleeping through it."

"Don't be silly. One of us needs to sleep, and you look like a sweet little boy when you do, so how could I wake you?"

"Boy, huh? I'll give you boy."

Damon gave a sexy growl and climbed on top of me, his morning wood pressing against his boxer briefs in a way that normally made me want to do things I'd blush to mention. But that morning, I just...

"Sorry, sorry. A headache, I know."

Damon climbed off me, but not before brushing my hair aside and kissing my forehead. His lips were warm and soft. Tears burned at the corners of my eyes, so I turned away.

"Go on now, you. Hurry back."

He returned a short time later, his head lowered and his shoulders slumped. Panic knocked against my breast. I hesitated to ask what was wrong.

"Everything... okay?"

"Yeah, yeah. All good. Just — well, I guess Doug got an emergency call during the night. A client was upset about some mistake or something, so he had to drive to Connecticut to sort it out. We won't get to say goodbye, unfortunately."

"Oh... I'm sorry, babe. That's a shame."

The *coward*. Cowardly piece of shit. At least I wouldn't have to see his face. But I still had to figure out what to do. What *the hell* should I do? Tell Damon? Mel? Ruin everyone's happy existence? Nothing happened, not technically. Maybe... I *know*. I know, there's no excuse. No way to justify. If Dante hadn't bit him, would he have stopped? Does that even matter? I needed to be away from there, I needed clarity. Sitting up quickly, I made a decision, even though I knew it was as cowardly as Doug's.

"Hey, babe, maybe we should, you know, leave a little earlier than what we'd planned. Go check out some of the antique stores, get some photographs of the mountains...it'll be fun."

"You think Mel will mind? I told her we'd stay through dinner..."

"Nah, I'm sure she's ready to get her house back to normal. I'll tell her, and you pack our gear. Deal?"

"Whatever you say, Birdie. Hey, you okay? You seem...off."

"All good, babe. You worry too much. Now, get packing. I'll go find Mel."

I jump up from the bed and grab my robe.

"Oh, she's in the barn."

I froze, the color drained from my face.

"Whoa, babe. Sit down. What just happened to you? You're as white as this sheet."

"I— no, I just...got up too fast. That headache. I'm fine now. Really, I am."

I laughed to show him I was totally fine, then left the room before he could question me further. *I am the coward.* Unable to tell him what happened. Though I had no reason to be— I know this, intellectually — I was ashamed.

There was selflessness to my cowardice, though. This is what I'd convinced myself in those pre-dawn hours. Telling meant hurting the people I loved most. Telling meant everyone's life would be forever changed. Destroyed. *I'm strong*, I told myself. I can bear the burden, and spare Damon and Mel. I can keep the disgusting secret, keep us away from Doug, keep Damon's delusion intact.

My thinking was marred by shock, but I hadn't fully realized it until later. Much later. By then it was too late, I didn't know how to say what should've been said to the two of them that morning.

Even when the opportunity arose, a short time later, I chickened out. I h almost walked into Mel as she was exiting the barn, a full bucket of goat's milk in one hand.

"Hey, Damon said I'd find you out here. Need a hand?"

STILL HERE

"Good morning, sunshine. How's your head?"

"Good. Better. All better now. Listen, how would you feel about us taking off a little earlier today than planned? Like, a lot earlier... an hour or two from now, to be exact."

"Oh, sure, Doug leaves, and now you want to hightail it out of here, too, huh? I see how it is."

"No! No, it's not like that at all, I – we..."

"Settle down, kid, settle down. Jumpy, much? I'm teasing you. I totally understand. You guys have a window of opportunity. You've got *freedom* right now. Go, enjoy. Live it up. Once you start popping out the rug rats, party's over, momma."

"Oh, please, you love it. And it's looking more and more like an *if*, not a when for us." I attempted to redirect the subject.

"Where are the twins, anyhow?"

"Stop, it'll happen when the time is right. Oh, and Mommy of the Year right here is letting them watch The Jungle Book. Again. It's the only way I can get anything done. Don't judge me."

"Me, judge you? Please. *If,* and *when* Damon and I have kids, they'll probably be having Pop Rocks for breakfast and watching Texas Chainsaw Massacre before they're five."

We laughed and kept bouncing terrible parenting ideas off each other. Then Mel stopped.

"Hey, did you— did you happen to see Doug at all last night? Like, during the night, I mean."

My heart stuttered, and I broke into a cold prickly sweat. Blood rushed to my head, sounding like the surf raging in my ears.

"What? Doug? Last night? I..."

To my own ears, I sounded guilty, my voice shrill.

"It's just, well he mentioned he couldn't sleep and he'd gone out to the barn. Dante *bit* him by the way. Hysterical, right? And I saw footprints in the wet grass from the balcony to the barn when I woke up this morning. I thought— I don't know, I guess I was hoping you saw him."

"H—hoping?" I stammered.

"Yeah, he was acting weird. All week, now that I think about it. Haven't you noticed?"

This is the moment. *Tell her.*

"Wh— I...no. Nope, can't say I have. Sorry."

"Huh. He's probably just stressed about work. Sorry I even mentioned it."

"Don't be silly!"

I could see the embarrassment flush her cheeks, so I changed the subject again. This time it worked. Inside, we found Damon just as I'd expected. The Jungle Book was on high volume, and all three shoveled chocolates into their mouths.

"See, this is what I was telling you. Candy before ten a.m."

"Aw, c'mon. A little chocolate never hurt anyone, ladies."

"Damon Michael Harrison! Unless you plan on dealing with their sugar high, I suggest you get upstairs and grab our bags."

"Ha, spoken like a mom-in-training right there."

We all laughed, but underneath the laughter there was uncertainty. A delicacy, if you will. Damon and I have been trying for two years to have a child.

Had been trying for years. I guess it's safe to say that won't be happening now.

NINE
A CHANGE

Winds in the east, mist coming in, / Like somethin' is brewin' and bout to begin. / Can't put me finger on what lies in store, / But I fear what's to happen all happened before.
Bert, Mary Poppins

It's September. Four months since I've died. Four months of watching and following Damon with a helpless longing. Around the house and up and down the almost deserted beach. He jogs for miles and miles, sneakers pounding the packed sand close to the shore. I run beside him.

I suppose, as a ghost, I could hover and float. But no, I do like I've always done. Mostly. I can't open doors or refrigerators, turn on the television or drink a glass of wine. I just kind of... *am*. One moment I'm on this side of a door then, *poof*, I'm on the other.

So, I do the things I used to do, minus those I can't. True, I'd hoped by now I'd have something more exciting to say, something more *dynamic*. But it's just another day here in the dead world.

STILL HERE

Waiting... for something. A sign, a command, or I don't know, a mission. A *purpose*. There's got to be a purpose for this, right? But what is it? What if there *is* no purpose or reason? What if I never know? I'd thought my reason for being was Damon, but I've yet to do anything to help him. Perhaps this is all there is, but I can't imagine living trapped behind the mirror, watching Damon's life go on without me.

The longer I stay, the less I'm able to let go of what was once mine. I don't care if it's childish or unfair. I still get to run on the beach with him at dawn and dusk, sit across from him as he eats breakfast. I still get to sleep beside him at night. Watch his chest rise and fall, his long dark lashes flutter on his cheeks as he dreams.

He still falls asleep as though I'm in the crook of his arm, so I tuck my body against him, my hand splayed on his chest. Sometimes— and I blush as I confess this— but, sometimes I run my hand down his torso, my ring finger tracing the vertical crease down his center, slip my hand inside his boxers and wrap around his heat, just how I had when I was alive and wanted to rouse him. Sometimes, when his sleep is fitful, he remains soft, vulnerable.

Other nights, when his sleep is deep, and my hand wraps around him, he becomes hard and I stroke him. I'd be lying if I said I've not climbed on top of him, felt him hard against my core, and rocked against his hardness. In his deepest sleep, Damon can feel me. His strong hands hover at the phantom swell of my hips, and his move in slow circles and thrusts. His lips part, my name sighs from them. Tears slip from his closed eyes.

Does he know I'm here, or does his brain tell him it's but a dream? No matter, when the night has passed, and the dawn greets us cruelly, it is with devastation anew and abounding. And his life, or the semblance of, goes on.

He wakes, brushes his teeth and showers. Uses the toilet, washes his hands, slicks back his curls, unrulier than ever, and goes downstairs. Puts on the coffee pot—the old-fashioned percolator kind, the only one we'd ever used—and checks his emails on his phone. Ignores the voicemails and the texts. They're fewer now, the ones checking how he's *doing*, if he *needs* anything, that he should *come out* one night, buddy.

The casserole brigade has long ceased, as have the flood of sympathy cards in our mailbox. The only constant is Claire's daily calls or texts. He answers most; she's hurting, too, after all. He brings the coffee and his laptop to the back deck and stares with unseeing eyes out at the restless ocean.

"We need to go back to the island, Damon."

It is a one-sided conversation. One of many I have at him. But this, a return to the island, I've been thinking this almost incessantly. He doesn't react. Not that I expect him to, of course. But as soon as the words touch the air, I know I am right. We must go back to the island where I died, and I *must* find the boy. The little black boy with the knowing eyes, who may or may not hold the answers to my questions.

"Happy Birthday, Birdie."

I startle, not because Damon has spoken aloud to me. He still does this with no less frequency as I do him, and as he had in the beginning days of my deadness. I startle because it's my birthday. September twenty-fourth. I'm thirty-eight. Or I would be. Does aging stop when you die? I've no idea. I'd ask someone on this side, but there's no one. Not a single fucking one. I'm behind the damn one-way mirror all the time; I can see out, but no one can see in. It's awful, but I'm used to it. Damon continues.

"How should we celebrate today, my love? How about a lovely jump off the pier?"

My head jerks up— I'd been looking down at his hands, I've always loved his hands. Artist hands, they are. Broad palms, long fingers. And even though I know he can't hear me, I say...

"Don't even think about it, buddy."

He says along with me. He knows that is what I'd say to such a suggestion.

"It's supposed to be getting easier, Birdie. That's what everyone says, you know. *'It'll get easier, man,'* and *'time is the healer of all things.'* They're wrong, babe. They're so fucking wrong. I feel you everywhere, I can *smell* you still. I swear to God, at night..."

He stops, clears his throat, then grabs his coffee with a shaking hand and tries to take a sip. It sloshes onto the deck, and he set it back down. He puts his head in his hands, elbows hard against his knees and his fingers grip his hair as he rocks on his heels. His agony kills me. Well... you know. I can't joke right now.

I do what I can only do, even though it can bring him no comfort. I stand behind my sweet, sad Damon. Rest my hands on his warm, bare shoulders and press my lips to his hair, between his laced fingers. His hair smells like sleep and ocean, like *home*. He doesn't so much stiffen as pause. One hand slips from his hair and falls carefully to his shoulder, over mine. *On* mine. I stare in shock; his hand is on mine. Slowly, as if afraid to scare a skittish kitten, Damon leans back in his chair until his head rests against my diaphragm, just below and between the swell of my breasts. With the same cautious, slow movement, I raise my other hand to his curls and massage his scalp in slow circles.

We stay like this as the sun brightens the sky. Silent, cautious, disbelieving but hopeful. I can't see his face, but I know silent tears are rolling down his beard—rough cheeks and his jaw is clenching and unclenching rhythmically. I won't speak this time. I will take this birthday gift and be grateful. Has it been ten minutes, or two? Time is standing still, as still as we are. But then, life interrupts.

Damon's phone buzzes and vibrates on the table, causing him to jump. He makes to squeeze my hand, keep the moment alive, but it's clear, he only feels the air on his shoulder now.

TEN
LIMBO

"Well, sir, if things are real, they're there all the time." "Are they?" said the Professor; and Peter did not quite know what to say.
—C.S. Lewis, The Lion, the Witch and the Wardrobe

I've stopped expecting rhyme or reason to this limbo. At least, that's what I tell myself. Between *those* times, I yell at the sky and shout into the night sky.

'*What is the meaning of this?*' and
'*What do you want me to do?*'

It's to no avail. Damon is floundering. Quietly, solitarily drowning in his private grief and confused hope. I continue to watch, helpless and waiting for another connection that may not even come.

My clothes are still in the closet, my drawers are still full. My shampoo and conditioner still in the shower. There's a bottle of store-bought kombucha in the fridge I'd gotten with every intention of drinking. Purchased one week before our trip to the island. I'd taken one sip and found it disgusting.

"It's got ginger, babe. You don't like ginger," Damon had reminded me the day I brought it home.

I'd insisted, though.

"I'll drink it, don't worry. Geez."

It's still on the top shelf, next to the coconut milk, and I see his eyes shift to it, then away, every time he opens the stainless-steel door.

"Throw it *away*, babe. C'mon."

It remains. It's been eight months now, that I've been gone-*ish*. The weird little time hops have slowed in frequency, but they still occur at random. It's like we're a video being fast—forwarded and paused by an unattended child.

Christmas and New Year have gone by. The holidays, much to our respective surprise, were happy...*ish*. The parts I saw, at least. This, thanks to an unexpected visitor to Birdie's Nest. Damon had been in the shower when the doorbell's melodic chimes rang through the house.

"Hang on, hang on! I'm coming."

Under his breath, he muttered, "Who the hell is at our door on Christmas Eve?"

Damon, hair and torso dripping, wrapped one of our thick sea green towels low around his waist and trotted down the stairs. He'd been planning on staying in, despite Claire's wishes for him to join her and Daddy for the week in St. Croix.

"A whim," she'd said with a shrug and forced nonchalance. "Time for a new tradition, perhaps," she added.

She didn't have to say it. It was too painful to be in the house where they'd spend every holiday celebration since I'd been born. For Damon, he couldn't imagine being anywhere *but* here, in our little house by the sea. Alone.

"Jesus, you'll break the damn... Aiden?"

Damon had swung the door open, pausing and widening his eyes at who waited on the other side.

"Jesus. Aiden. Lord Voldemort... I answer to all. Shit, you look awful, and yet scrumptious, too. Hmm. Here, champagne. Do you drink champagne, even? No matter, I do. Are you going to invite me in, or...?"

"Right, yeah, of course. You just — just caught me off guard. We — I haven't seen you since..."

"Yes. Well, you know."

The two men — my husband and my lifelong best friend — looked off in different directions. The funeral, of course. By the way, if anyone *ever* says, '*Gee, I'd kinda like to be a fly on the wall at my own funeral, just to see who turns up,*' tell them to shut up. Just stop. You don't want to see that. Trust me.

"So, how long you in town for? How come you didn't call?"

"A week, maybe more, maybe less. Richard and I are...well, we're on a break. He says I've become '*distant*.' I'm *grieving*, damn it. Why doesn't anyone *understand* that?"

Aiden clenched his fists and shook them at the ceiling dramatically, then sighed.

"Anyhow, I stood pathetically alone in my kitchen, pouring a tall gin and tonic. You know, indulging in my pity party for one, and it hit me. *'Damon would know how I feel!' You* understand. All too well, I see *now*," he added, appraising Damon's thinned frame.

"Are you going to open it, or…"

Damon looked down at the bottle, then his watch.

"It's, uh, 9:15, buddy."

Aiden rolled his eyes as if to say *'amateur.'*

"Um, hello? Mi*mosas*, they're a morning drink, thank you. Give it to me. I know where everything is. Unless you've…"

"No, everything is where… it should be."

Everything is where I put it. That's what he was about to say, they both knew this. I was giddy with happiness to see my two men together. Their friendship, born from a mutual love for me, was a sweet surprise. Before I'd introduced them, I'd given them respective warnings.

To Aiden:

"Now, you be *nice*. Damon is different. He's special, okay?"

"You offend me, darling. I am *always* nice, thank you very much."

"Have you forgotten what you said to *me* when we first met?"

"Oh, please, we were *nine*, for heaven's sake. And your nose *was* slightly too long. And you *were* too short. You were like a little long-nosed nugget. What? God, you've grown into your nose, even if you're still a nugget."

"This is what I'm talking about. You don't have to say everything that comes into your head. Aid, I think — no, I know — I'm in love with him. He's sweet and sensitive, and brilliant. And gorgeous, too."

"Oh, so you need me to use my gaydar to see if he pitches for my team or yours, hmm?"

"Oh, my God. Stop, no. Your opinion matters to me. *You* matter to me. If you two don't hit it off..."

"Oh, sweet pea, relax. If he's everything you say he is — and I'm sure he is — then we'll get on famously. But if he *is* all that, and happens to swing my way, I'm stealing him. Just saying, sweetie."

To Damon:

"I want you to meet someone very important to me, like, as important as my parents. His name is Aiden, and he's been my best friend since we were nine years old."

"Okay, Birdie. How about we grab some tickets for a game and invite him and his girl?"

"Well, about that. It would have to be tickets for a show, and for him and his *guy*."

Damon blinked a moment, his head cocked and brow creased. Then he smiled and nodded.

"Ohhh, gotcha. So, what show you think they'd like?"

My love solidified at that moment. When the two met, there was none of the typical straight guy/gay guy awkwardness. Damon laughed and shrugged at Aiden's very gay innuendos and teasing flirtations. Aiden pretended to follow Damon's dissertations on the beauty of team sports, IPA's, and tent camping. They became, and have remained, friends. Even after I've gone.

The men, after Aiden poured them their mimosas — heavy on the champagne, light on the orange juice — went out to the living room. Damon lit the gas fireplace, and they sat in the two worn leather chairs that faced it. I sat, invisible to them, on the hearth, watching their faces and the gray sky out the French doors. The silence was companionable. All three of us lost in our respective reveries as a light snow began to fall over the beach.

"I keep expecting to see one of her ridiculous cat memes pop up on my phone. I mean, she never even liked cats."

Damon smiled and nodded. I laughed. That was our 'thing,' me and Aiden. Memes and gifs, all day long. We once had a running 'emoji' text conversation, no words allowed. We even tried to include Damon once, but he couldn't keep up with our silly rapid-fire responses and gave up.

"You two drove me nuts with that," Damon chuckled.

Aiden slid far forward in his seat, almost spilling his drink with the sudden movement. He leaned closer to Damon.

"Do you ever feel like she's...*here*?"

He swept his hand around the room to emphasize as if it weren't clear. Damon didn't answer right away. I studied his face, knowing a debate wage behind his eyes. Should he say 'yes' and share his secret world? Tell Aiden that even though his *heart* believes, his mind insists he's crazy to think that yes, I *am* still here? Would he confess he feels me curled up against him at night, and sometimes holding his hand? Could he tell Aiden he has felt my lips against the pulse in his throat, my hand around his... Or should he lie, and say no? Before he could answer, Aiden, his voice halting, clarified.

"I don't mean like a ghost '*here.*' Just like, I don't know. Her spirit? Like, her essence. Or something."

He exhaled, dropped back against the backrest, took a long, hand—trembling sip from his glass, then went on.

"I'm sorry. It's just, I've been thinking about her *so* much. You know she was what made growing up a gay boy in suburbia bearable. Did she ever tell you about the time she beat up Johnny Misner for calling me a faggot? Then, when he was on the ground, clutching his bloody nose, she told him that when she died, she was coming back to haunt him for the rest of his life." He let out a small laugh. "Who even *says* that? Taylor, that's who. God, when we were kids, she was always talking about death, the little weirdo. She had all these, I don't know, ideas about '*the afterlife.*' First, she decided that when she died, she'd be a ghost. I told her she was cliché. I wasn't even sure what cliché meant at the time, but it felt right to me. *Then* she said she was going to be reincarnated. I said, '*what if you come back as, like, a lobster, or something else crappy*'? But you know our girl: stubborn as the proverbial mule. She'd 'decided.' That's what she said. *Decided.* As if she had a say in the matter!"

Aiden fell back into his chair and slumped down. He pressed his trembling chin to his chest, trying to keep it still. Damon stayed quiet, knowing Aiden needed to unburden.

"Oh, and then, af—after she read Jonathan Livingston Seagull, she decided her whole philosophy was going to be based on *that*. Damn—damned if I can remember what the hell it was about, though. Something about reaching higher planes, or whatever. You know what I said to all that?"

Aiden took a shuddering breath, and through restrained sobs, he spat out, "Dead is *dead*. They stick you in the gr- ground, you-you decay, you are *dirt*."

He put his hand over his eyes, and his shoulders shook with almost silent tears.

"Why the fuck did I say that to her? That's a fucking *horrible* thing to say. She just wanted to believe…"

"She's here."

Silence, but for the small, shuddering sniffs from Aiden. His head turned on a slow swivel. It was almost comical, were it not for his tear-streaked face and reddened eyes. Aiden raised an eyebrow at Damon. I watched him too. Damon stared into the fire, his unchecked tears leaving trails down his cheeks. He took another sip of his mimosa. This, too, would have otherwise struck me as comical. Damon holding the dainty fluted glass, but the weighted suspense held any laughter at bay.

Aiden, with great effort, pulled himself upright again and sat at the edge of his chair. With the same theatrical movements, he set his emptied glass on the small table between them. Then, he clasped his hands together like a steeple and rested them against his chin.

"You mean...like...*here* here?"

Aiden punctuated the question with a dramaturgical look around the room. This corner and that, the ceiling, the mantle. Then his eyes, still bright from crying, lit up and a smile transformed his face. I knew what he was about to say before he said it.

"Is she like, Marion Kerby? Oh, *say* she's like Marion Kerby!"

Damon blinked at him with blank eyes, so he added in his most exasperated tone, "*Topper*! Oh, heaven help me," he pinched the bridge of his nose, and put his other hand skyward, then continued, "Cary *Grant*. Constance *Bennett*. Top—*per*. Taylor's favorite Cary Grant movie. Right after Bringing Up Baby, The Bishop's Wife, and just before Holiday, that is. I *know* she made you watch it."

"Oh, that's right! I remember now."

Damon slapped his knee and gave a short burst of laughter. The first real one I'd heard from him since I died. His smile lingered, I'd bet he was thinking about all the old movies I used to make him watch. Topper, and Topper Returns, His Girl Friday, The Philadelphia Story, and so many more. Bringing Up Baby was my favorite, though. I'd watched it fifteen times, twice with him. He surprised me on our wedding night with the band playing, for their last song, "I Can't Give You Anything But Love, Baby." We danced alone on the faded wood dance floor. Twinkling lights draped low from the rafters of the old barn. Ivory sweetheart rose petals from my bouquet lay scattered like snow. The sepia photograph upon the mantle captured the moment. It was... *magical.*

"You haven't answered me, Damon. What exactly do you mean, *she's here*?"

"I don't know how to explain it, man. Birdie's just... here. I know she is."

"So, does she, like, talk to you?"

"No — not like, no. It's like she — I can feel her, okay? Can we leave it at that?"

"Oh. My. God. Damon Michael Harington, are you having... *ghost sex*?"

He whisper-hissed the last two words, then covered his gaping mouth dramatically. He was back to his usual campy self again. Then he added,

"Is it good? No, don't tell me. Of *course*, it's good. Ghost sex is *hot*. Now, dish. Tell me what you and our naughty little ghost girl are up to."

"What is wrong with you?"

"What? Come on, you can tell Uncle Aiden. Oh, fine. Never mind."

He picked at an imaginary pill on his sweater, then slyly, he said,

"Wanna have a séance? Before you say no..."

"No, definitely not."

"Okay, but my psychic says..."

"You have a psychic?"

"I'm gay. *Yes*, I have a psychic."

"Is that a thing?"

"No, you ninny. I'm kidding. At least I think I am. Anyhoo—my psychic says people who die unexpectedly usually linger around their loved ones. Like, trying to give them comfort and, I don't know, closure or something. So they can move on, or whatever. I've been trying to reach our girl for months now. I know she has a message for me. Oh, you too, of course."

He said this as an afterthought, as he flicked through his phone.

"Where is her number, damn it? Her name is Sheila — *Madam* Sheila. But I *refuse* to call her that—and she charges a very reasonable-ish rate for home visits."

Damon had already tuned him out and was just waiting for him to wind himself down. Me, on the other hand? Well, I started jumping up and down with excitement. If I were alive, the pictures on the mantle would be rattling. But, since I'm not, there's no register of my jumps. Except...

"Is there a window open?"

Damon looks around, "No, why?"

"The fire is all...wonky." Aiden gasped, "Do you think its Taylor, telling us she's here? Oh, my God! Taylor honey? Tay—Tay, It's me. Aiden. Give me a sign you are here."

He said this very slow, annunciating his words the way an idiot might talk to a deaf person, or a non-English speaking foreigner, instead of a dead woman. I — and this is childish, I know — I went up close to his face and said,

"Ooooooo—ooooOOOoooo."

Nothing, no reaction. Not that I was expecting one, of course. I sighed.

"No worries, Aiden, my friend. You're not the only one who doesn't hear me."

I gave his cheek a pat. Aiden gasped and put his hand on his face, right where I'd touched him. Well,

I'll be damned! Damon watched him, an eyebrow arched, yet now, he too leaned forward.

"What? Did you — did she..."

Aiden gasped again, this time at Damon.

"She *is* here! I knew it, I just *knew* it."

Then his eyes softened, seeing Damon as if for the first time.

"You poor thing, you. *This* is why you don't go out. Isn't it?"

"I go out."

Damon squirmed, uncomfortable under the imagined spotlight over his chair.

"I leave the house, man. All the time."

"You go to the store. The beach. And... where else? Nowhere. Your friends — Charlie and Jack — they say you haven't been out to visit him since... before."

Damon gave him an incredulous look.

"You've talked to Charlie? *And* Jack?"

Aiden shrugged and looked at anything but Damon.

"Social media, *God*. You're like the only one not on there, Damon. We've all talked. All except for that Doug. He never responded the creep. Sorry, I never... well, Claire called, too. That's how I knew you were home. Who turns down St. Croix, by the way?"

"Everyone needs to just... not worry about me. I'm fine. It's only been..."

"It's fast approaching a year, Damon. And I'm not judging, not at all. But... I don't know if this is *healthy*. You're still alive Damon, and Taylor would want you to..."

"Please, don't. Don't say Birdie *'would want me to keep living, fall in love again,'* and all that crap. Birdie would want to be *here*, damn it. Alive, with me, living the life we planned. We planned this life, here. *Together*. She *is* still here, Aiden, and I am *not* going anywhere. You understand? I'm not going to leave her behind. Ever."

Aiden sat contritely. Damon's face reddened, his free hand gripped the arm of the chair. A small sniff from Aiden was enough to soften his tone and loosen his grip.

"Sorry, but I just want everyone to leave me alone on this. I know how I look, okay? Like a sad sack. Pathetic, maybe even a little crazy, but I don't care."

He reached across the side table and grasped Aiden's arm, who looked both close to tears and ready to jump out of his skin.

"I know you mean well, buddy. But you said it yourself — you feel it, she *is* here. So, tell me Aid — if the one and only love of your life was still somehow with you, even after death — what would *you* do?"

Aiden tilted his head at Damon and gave him that look, the one that says, 'oh, puh-lease.'

"Ex*actly* the same thing, darling."

Then, to the air, he called out,

"Tay—Tay, be a love, and refill our drinks, will you?"

He did a theatre-quality double take on Damon's expression and added, "What? It was worth a try. Geez. Give me your glass. Let's get plastered, what do you say? Merry fucking Christmas to us, right?"

The boys drank themselves silly. I didn't get to stay the whole time. Time hopped, I was fast-forwarded again. One moment I'm watching Damon and Aiden get slurring drunk on Christmas Eve. The next, I'm noting January's bleak arrival. Then, with a blink I'm here now, watching Damon sleep on the morning of his birthday, a month later. February twenty-second.

ELEVEN
RAGE

It looked as if a night of dark intent was coming, and not only a night, an age. Someone had better be prepared for rage...
—Robert Frost

The time and date glow brightly on Damon's phone. I start to smile, then it freezes on my lips as I glance around the room. Something isn't right. My chest tightens. Shards of broken glass and destroyed picture frames litter the bedroom carpet. There is a triangular dent midway up the wall, across from the bed. It's from the corner of one of those picture frames, I'm certain. My eyes next travel to another hole in the plaster. It's the size and shape of an oversized lemon. A fist. My head whips back around again at Damon. One arm is thrown over his face to block the morning light, and the other is stretched across my side of the bed. My pillow is askew, and his hand grips its corner. There's dried blood across his swollen knuckles.

What the hell happened here?

I spring from the bed and go out into the hallway to see what else, if anything, is in disarray. The hallway and bathroom are fine. The door to the spare bedroom, the one we've always used as a shared office, is open. Our desks are on opposite sides of the wide window that overlooks the ocean. His desk, the one seen first when entering the room, is as usual. Stacks of papers with handwritten notes and revisions on yellow sticky-notes poke from the piles. His Elvis '68 Comeback mug is by his laptop on the right side and a photograph of the suntanned version of us on the beach on the left. Above the laptop is another sticky note, this one is a reminder FINAL DRAFT DUE: MARCH 10. He's almost done writing his book. I smile, proud of him.

Everything is in order on his side, but mine is another story. Things are *not* as they've always been. My chair is overturned as if someone had risen abruptly, kicking it back with their calves. My laptop is open. It had been closed all this time, these nine months I've been dead. I'd never password protected it. I know in an instant what Damon has read. If my heart still beat, it would've sunk. It is the unsent letter I wrote to Doug.

'Doug,

For months now, I have kept silent, in hopes that you would somehow right this. But there's been nothing, no apology, no confession... nothing. Do you really think we can all go on as if things are okay?? You tried to rape me. You son of a bitch. How? How could you do that to me? To Damon? Your best friend. Do you have any idea what this will do to him? Do you even care? We will never, ever come back to the farm again. I hate you for this. I hate you for destroying everything. And what about your WIFE, Doug? Does she know what kind of monster you are? You bastard. The only thing that keeps me silent is my fear of what this would do to them, to Damon and Mel, our SPOUSES. I don't care how you do it, but stay the fuck out of our lives.'

I never sent it. I typed it, then closed out the 'compose email' tab, wiped away angry tears and went back to my life. The message had automatically saved to my drafts, and Damon has seen it. I rush back to the bedroom on unstable legs, frantic now that the time thief will steal this moment away before I can attempt to reach Damon. He is just as I left him, arms slung over face and pillow.

"Damon? Babe, wake up. Listen to me…"

Damon lifts away the arm that covered his face, his eyes open. He turns his head to the sound of my voice.

"Birdie."

He hears me. Wait. He *sees* me.

"Babe, I…"

"Just — just come here. Quick, before you're gone again."

And I do, I hurry to his side of the bed and sit on the edge, facing him. He takes my hands in his —

not my ghost hands, but *my hands* — and presses them against his stubbled cheeks as he sits up. He takes my face the same way. With gentle reverence, he rubs my cheekbones with his thumbs while his fingers twine in my hair. We are both trembling, confused and unsure.

'I'm so sorry I didn't…"

"Shhh, shhh,"

He hushes me, turns his head aside and squeezes his eyes shut as his brow draws down. Then he turns back, opens them again and we are lost in each other's eyes, trying to say everything there is to say without words. We are both writers, and yet neither have the words to encompass the abounding waves of emotions. Words like love and longing are but pale, weak attempts to define a love like this.

The windows are closed to the noise of the sea, inside the house it is silent. The only sound to be heard is the caw of a lone seagull somewhere on the roof. Time has paused again, and no one has told the gull. Damon exhales a slow, shaky breath, and presses his forehead against mine. His hands are still in my hair, thumbs on my cheeks. He is afraid if he lets go, I'll be gone again. So am I. I'm afraid to do anything, but with his lips so close and his skin against mine, how can I not kiss him?

I don't so much as break contact as I shift it, so my forehead nudges his temple. Our lips are near touching, his breath on my mouth; short, hot puffs of air pass between my parted lips. I imagine Damon's air racing down my throat and filling my lungs. Giving me life. I trace his lower lip with my fingertips. We kiss. A soft press of warm lips, cautious.

But the moment our tongues touch, the familiar fire erupts between us. Damon frees his hands from my hair and wraps them around my waist, pulling my willing body on top of his as he lay back on the bed. Our kisses have not diminished in intensity but have traveled from mouths, to throats, to breast, and bicep. Every inch must be covered, consumed.

We question nothing at this moment; not why, or how, or even how long. We accept what *is*. We make love as if the world might end, because, for us, it may. Again. It is both parts a cruelty and kindness, this interlude. But will it last?

So far, it does. Morning has become noon, and the weak February sun filters through the sheer curtains. Damon's bare leg is strewn possessively over my hip, our fingers twined, my head tucked into the crook of his neck. I am as impossibly alive as I am certainly dead. I feel, but my cursed heart does not beat. He can hear, see and feel me, but we know. In our heart of hearts, we know.

There's something I need to say to him, but I'm hesitating. I must tell him we need to go back to the island, that *I* must find the boy. I *know* this. But I fear that if I do—if I say the words—I'll vanish from him again the moment he's heard them. He shifts, and takes my hand in his and kisses my palm. I know he's about to speak, the extra inhalation, the heavy exhalation, is his tell.

"How?"

"I don't know, babe."

"How long?"

I shake my head against his shoulder. He sighs again. Is he debating whether to ask about Doug? Wondering, should he taint this moment with speaking words about a thing that cannot be undone or unknown? No.

"I love you, Birdie. With every ounce of my body and my soul, I love you. You knew... you know that, right?"

"Always."

And then I grin against the hollow between his neck and shoulder, and say what I would've when I was alive and after he'd say the most romantic things,

"Ditto."

His chest bounces with his laughter, but the laugh turns to a shudder and restrained sob.

"*Fuck*, Birdie. Why..." he roughly wipes his eyes with his palm, "...why the fuck did this have to happen to us? And what the hell *is* happening?"

But I have no answers for him. No ghostly been-to-the-other-side wisdom passed from the lips of God to my ear. No sudden infinite knowledge or serenity to offer. I don't know either. So, instead of answering, I raise my face to his and kiss away the tear that has escaped and slid down his cheek. I can taste the saltiness.

I am still here.

"You must be starving," I say instead.

"I'm afraid to move from this spot. What if..."

"I know. Me, too."

"Birdie?"

I wait. Damon steadies his voice.

"I don't know how I... I don't know how to go on without you. Is this my fault you're stuck? Am I... forcing you to stay because I can't let go?"

My heart (the traitor) aches at his torment.

"I'm where I want to be, babe. If anything, *I'm* the one who can't let go. I worry that I'm forcing you to live like... like a zombie."

He tousles my hair. A gesture from the good old alive days when I'd say something he found silly or unworthy of correction for its absurdity.

"Then we're both where we want to be. It's settled. I'm a zombie, married to a ghost. Perfect."

But we know it's not perfect. We know. Who could blame us, though, for taking this precious and surreal gift?

"I'm afraid I'll..."

"Don't say it. I'm afraid, too. Let's just," he rolls over, on top of me, "take what we have, for as long as we have it."

And this is the essence of how to *live*, isn't it? The irony does not escape me, of course. His hip bones, sharper now than ever before, press into my flesh. He grows hard between my legs, and I raise my hips to him and pull his body against mine. We make love again, postponing what I must tell him to do.

I suppose it's like I'm trying to pull a fast one on the universe (God?) by not saying what I'm given a chance to say. The longer I wait, the more time I'm given. It's a bold and risky move; what if they (whoever they are) tire of my stalling and whisk me away again. But what if I get to stay? Maybe God, the universe, or *they* have realized there's been a terrible cosmic mistake in taking me away from Damon. Perhaps his suffering is more than even they can bear.

I'm absurd, I know. Damon and I, we are no more aggrieved, no more robbed of happiness than anyone else who's lost a loved one. To presume so is a cruel slap to anyone who has ever lost a child, a partner, a parent. Our love, as great as it is to *us*, is no greater than someone's else's.

When I was alive, I believed it was. I marveled and rejoiced at how amazing our love was. How perfectly imperfect and special. How magical and blessed. How prideful and boastful it was to say and think such things. I not only tempted fate, but I also taunted it like a child teasing a hungry dog with a treat. Then the dog finally lunged and tore our life to shreds. Where I regarded our love as a grand prize, Damon cultivated it like a rare jewel, a unicorn. *He* was humble, gracious.

I press tighter against him. *He doesn't deserve this, damn it.* I'm angrier for him than myself. This is bullshit. Maybe *I* deserved it— sin of pride and all— but Damon? He's done nothing, *ever* to deserve this. Go ahead and think I'm full of shit, or naïve, or something. But I mean this with complete sincerity: Damon is as close to perfection as any human can get.

Were he not so genuine, it would've driven me a little nuts, how great he was. *Is*. When we were out somewhere, and I'd unkindly give someone a once over and say, *'wow, somebody dressed with the lights off today.'* Damon would give me *that look—*

the one where he tips his head to the side and raises his eyebrow. Then give me a gentle admonishment.

'Now, Birdie, we have no idea what his circumstances are.' Then he'd lighten his chastisement (to spare me shame) and add with a smile, *'Maybe he's colorblind. Or something.'*

When I'd become annoyed at the drive-thru clerk and swear about *'how fucking hard can it be to make a damn coffee with one cream and one sugar'* he'd respond,

'Birdie, they probably can't hear very well over those headsets. Be nice.'

Then, whenever I'd get haughty and offended when someone wasn't as well-mannered or polite as *I* think everyone should be,

'Sweetheart, we have no idea what's going on in their world right now. Maybe their dog just died or something.'

Damon would always soften his rebuke, so it didn't come across as condescending or harsh. It made me always want to do better, *be* better. And punch him. Kidding. I'm just kidding. It's really quite a gift, to be able to wrap a reprimand in sugar and feed it to someone in a way that makes them want to eat their own words. I'm glad he has it, that he's always known how to use it.

Damon could do that with anyone. Once, while we were in a restaurant, a couple at a table near us got into a loud, heated argument. The young manager approached them. As he twisted his ring and darted his eyes around, he spoke in a low tone. He'd intended to hush them with as little attention draw as possible. But the very large man turned his wrath on him. His wife was no better, waving her arms at and berating both men and anyone daring to look at them.

Against my wishes, Damon stood, set his beer down and approached the table. He placed a hand on the large man's shoulder. I cringed in anticipation of his reaction. Then he whispered something in the manager's ear. The manager, who couldn't have been much more than twenty—five, nodded almost convulsively and shuffle—ran behind the bar, shooing the bartender out of his way.

Damon returned his attention to the couple. The man I could see only in profile. The woman was in full view, though. Her voluminous black hair fanned out from her boldly made-up face, and red lipstick extended past her lip line by a mile. She watched Damon with *the look*. The one women usually got when Damon spoke to them, doe-eyed and swoony. The man, at first stiff-postured and glaring, suddenly laughed and shook Damon's hand. They, all three, turned and waved to me. The woman called out over three table lengths,

"Ya got yaself a sweetheart, don'tcha!"

I struggled not to laugh, all the while trying to ignore the stares of the entire restaurant. Damon winked and continued to chat with the couple until the manager returned with an uncorked bottle of wine. At last, he took his leave from the now happy couple.

"What on *earth* did you say?"

"Oh, well. I just told my new friend Tony he just saved my ass and I'd like to buy him and his bride a bottle of wine."

"Go on..."

Damon chuckles and shrugs.

"I said you were about to chew my head off for staying out all night, but got distracted by their argument. So the least I could do was buy them a drink."

"You are too much," I smiled and shook my head.

"Don't smile too much, remember, you're furious with me."

"Impossible."

"Good."

This is the kind of man Damon is. Kind, compassionate, thoughtful. He is a diffuser of tempers, soother of souls, a friend to all. Even when he lost his cool, though it happened rarely, it could be justified. God, this reads like a memorial... and I'm the dead one. Sorry, there's that gallows humor again. Anyhow, I can count all three times I've seen Damon lose it. The first incident:

The time we were on the Crystal River for a manatee swim excursion. The boat captain — a salty older man who's looks reminded me of the actor Gerald McRaney — kept calling me Blondie and sweetheart. Alone, it wasn't enough to do more than irritate Damon.

We had a simple understanding of these types of things that can be summed up by three words: *you handle it*. Meaning, if a guy was hitting on me, Damon expected me to handle the situation. If a woman was hitting on him, I expected *him* to handle the situation. See, simple.

The swim had gone wonderfully. We — us and eight strangers — were having fun. The manatees were magical with their silly fat, trunkless, elephant-like bodies and docile natures. But the boat captain was still paying an inordinate amount of attention to me. Calling out from the boat's deck helpful tips like, *'Swim to your left, Blondie, there's a manatee right over there,'* and giving little attention to anyone else.

None of this caused more than a head shake from Damon and a shrugging laugh from me. When our time was up, and the captain called us all back to the boat, I reluctantly returned, last to board. Captain Kinda-McCraney extended his hand to assist me up the steps, and as I cleared the threshold, he gave an extra little pull, and I stumbled against him. He slung a sinewy arm around my waist, and leered,

"Good thing for me you don't have your sea legs, Blondie."

I used my palms to push off from his sweat sheathed chest, half smiling, half grimacing, and retorted with an arched eyebrow,

"Well, thank goodness you're such a… *gentleman.*"

I took my spot beside Damon.

"Do you think he understands sarcasm," I whispered in his ear.

Despite his placid expression, his flaring nostrils and balled fists were enough warning to understand he was seething. Perhaps another man would've gotten up right then and knocked the captain on his ass, and he wouldn't be blamed. But Damon is a man who was born to a man like that, and he was not his father's son.

"Babe, it's handled. He's just an old dog playing old tricks," I whispered again.

Damon said nothing. I tried twice more, but his mouth was set in a hard line, his posture stony, and his eyes kept hidden by his sunglasses. When the captain docked the long pontoon boat, and the passengers filed off, I stood to exit as well, but Damon did not. I cocked my head, my brow creased.

"Babe?"

"Go on ahead, Birdie."

"*Babe.*"

"Go... please."

I sighed and put my hands on my hips. We were the last ones on the boat. The others were trudging along the weathered dock with their heavy wetsuits and gear.

"Hey Blondie, you wanna go for another..."

Damon tore off his sunglasses and was up and across the boat's deck so fast I hadn't time to react. Neither had the captain. He shoved the man, once, hard enough to rattle the frame of the covered deck. His tan, strong forearm was across the captain's throat, their faces inches apart. Damon, in a deathly low voice, said one word:

"Apologize."

"Whoa, buddy! I was just..."

"Apologize."

Damon's free hand curled into a fist. The captain raised his hands in submission.

"Alright, alright! Blon— miss, I apologize if I was out of line. Just havin' a little fun..."

Damon released him, and the captain wilted, letting out the breath he'd been holding. Without another word to him, Damon walked away. To me he said,

"Got everything?"

I nodded, my eyes wide and my heart racing. Then I dared a glance at the captain. His face was blotchy and his wary eyes slanted as he watched Damon. One hand balled into a fist, the other rubbed his throat, where Damon's arm had been.

Damon took my hand in his and guided me off the boat. We strode across the dock to our Jeep, his spine straight and his stride forced casual. I was speechless. I'd never seen him that angry before, nor use physical force to make his point. I confess I was both discomfited... and turned on. Once we were in the Jeep, I ventured a comment.

"So, uh...that was kinda hot, babe."

Sure, I meant it, but I was also trying to be funny. He wasn't ready to be amused.

"Birdie, I wanted — I *want* to punch his fucking face in. Beat the living shit out of him. Pound him into the ground. I don't think you understand how badly I want to do that, and how much restraint it is taking me not to go back there."

My hand hovered for a moment before resting on his arm. It was tense and rock hard from how tightly it was fisted in his lap. I knew where his torment lie. It wasn't about jealousy or possessiveness, it was about self-control and blind rage. It was about his father.

"Babe, you are not like him, you know that. *I* know that. You've proved it once again. You *didn't* punch him, you're not going back. You're here with me, your wife who wants to jump your bones right here and now."

A small smile, a sound that passed well enough as a laugh. The tendons in his arm began to even out again. I turned his face to mine. Smoothed away the crease in his forehead with my thumb. Then I slipped my fingers into his still damp hair and gently scratched his scalp. Damon closed his eyes and breathed in, then allowed himself to relax as he exhaled. He was letting me calm him down. Something I'm certain his father would never have let his mother do when they were alive. He has spoken of them only once, to give me a window into what has shaped him...

Evan Harrison, Damon's father, was a man of brilliant mind and violent tempers. Helena, his mother, was enigmatic, aloof, equally brilliant and just as fierce. They were both professors of the arts at a prestigious university. By day, they were charming and witty, by night combative and temperamental.

As their young, handsome son, Damon was trotted out to recite a sonnet or play a song on the piano at their questionably lavish and decadent university faculty parties. Then sent off to bed in the care of a nanny, who was usually some student trying to score points with either of the professors.

Their elitist and elegant life in the public eye was in stark contrast to the volatile private storms of their private life. Damon, an introverted, sensitive and genetically gifted child, spent his days caught between them. Helpless.

At nineteen he left for college across the country, as far from them as possible. At twenty—two, he was called home to identify their bodies. There had been a massive fire, cause suspicious but uncertain. Both parents had perished, the house burnt to the ground. With no other living family, Damon was alone in the world. His questions are forever unanswered. The atonement from his parents would never be realized. His forgiveness offered to a headstone in a cemetery.

The day after the funeral, he left from nothing and began his cross-country travels, writing along the way. He didn't return to college that semester or any after. At twenty-four, he was a twice over published author. The money that was left to him from his parents was donated to a domestic violence shelter.

The second incident:

There used to be an old homeless man by the pier near our house. Mellow Milo, we called him with great affection. Everyone knew Milo, and Milo knew everyone. He never begged for change or food. He insisted on 'earning' it. He'd sing a song in exchange for whatever you may have to give— and always refused offers of shelter or help. The town police (whose officers secretly delivered food and clothing to Milo on their own time) was willing to turn a blind eye, so long as he never caused trouble, and he never did. He was a beloved fixture. Damon was particularly affected by the diminutive man. Almost every morning, he would bring out two steaming cups of coffee for them to drink together.

I would watch them from the bedroom window. Damon's slow strides, his dark hair tousled by the ocean breeze, shirt billowing behind him as he carried the coffees across the pale sand. The small man, his slight frame frail and humped, reached up a grateful, trembling hand. Even from the balcony of our house, I could see his wide smile at my husband's approach. Damon in profile smiled down at his unlikely friend before sitting beside him. My heart swelled each time. They sometimes spoke, gesturing out at the sea or the sky, nodding their heads in understanding. Other times they sat silent, sipping strong coffee and greeting the new day in appreciative silence.

Then one midsummer evening, the unthinkable. With a storm threatening the coast, the beach stood deserted but for a handful of thrill-seeking teens and determined surfers. We'd stopped worrying too much about Milo. He seemed to always disappear to safety well before any inclement weather hit, only to reappear soon after the skies parted again.

Damon and I had decided to sit out on the balcony and watch the storm's approach. The sky curled and blackened in the distance. Flashes of lightning and rumbles of thunder trembled. A few fat drops of rain splattered on the rail and wood deck, a warning of what was to come. I was asking Damon something — I don't remember what — but he wasn't listening, his brow furrowed as he leaned forward. I followed his gaze towards the pier.

"What's wrong?"

"I'm not sure. Look — down by the pier. Are they…"

Several figures moved around on the sand under the pier. They almost looked as if they were dancing. Their arms raised and lowered, their legs flailing. I leaned forward as well, my brain understanding before my eyes did. Damon stood up, leaned over the balcony and squinted at the shapes a moment longer. Then he ran inside, down the stairs and out the back deck.

He sprinted across the beach, shouting. I started to follow him but then turned back for my phone. With a shaking hand, I dialed 911.

"911, what's you're emergency?"

"Yes," I panted, running towards the pier, "there's been an assault on the beach, please send someone!"

"What is your location, ma'am?"

"The pier — the one that's off Wyndemere drive. I think some kids have attacked Milo."

"Milo, ma'am?"

"Yes, the man — could you just send someone, please?"

By the time I'd reached Damon, the attackers had run off. Milo was an ominously still heap on the wet sand, curled in a fetal position. The tide was coming in, lapping at his bare foot. So Damon scooped him up in his strong arms as if he were a child and carried him up the beach, towards our house. I followed behind, my hand on the small of

Damon's back. As we reached the boardwalk, three cruisers and an ambulance arrived. The occupants sprang from the vehicles. A stretcher snapped open and wheeled over, the officers gingerly took the lifeless body from Damon's arms.

"Jesus, it *is* Milo. Poor old guy," said one.

"Did you see what happened? Can you identify the punks that did this, you think?" asked another.

"Sir, I'm going to need you to step back," said the EMT, his voice authoritative.

Damon was reluctant, so I took his arm. When I slid my hand down to take his, I saw the blood on his knuckles.

"I can identify one, at least. He'll be the guy with the busted-up face."

"You got ahold of one of 'em? Good. That's off the record, of course. I'm going to have to take you in for a statement, okay?"

"Wait, is Damon in trouble?"

"No, no. But, if we do find these guys, the one with the... facial reconstruction might want to press charges. Your husband's best defense is a strong offense. You might want to have a lawyer on hand."

Damon ignored all this. His eyes stayed trained on the medic and the old man on the stretcher.

"Is he... is he going to be alright?"

The medic, a young woman with prominent freckles and wide blue eyes, shook her head.

"I'm sorry, sir. He's deceased."

"No. You didn't perform CPR. Give him CPR."

"Sir, he has a DNR bracelet, legally, we can't. I'm sorry."

"Babe? Honey, I'm so sorry..."

Damon, his expression hard, turned to the officer, ignoring me.

"If you don't find those fuckers, I will."

"Sir — Mr..."

"Harrison," I finish.

"Mr. Harrison, I advise you to not say anything more."

"Damon, *please*."

My plea broke through his red haze of anger. He collected himself, giving the compassionate but firm officer a curt nod. Satisfied, he agreed to let us drive to the station after the storm. The cruisers and ambulance left. This time without sirens blaring, the lights strobed soundlessly. The sky opened, and Damon let me pull his head down to my shoulder, and I held him in the pouring rain.

We went back inside the house, stripped off our soaked clothes and went upstairs to our bathroom. I drew a bath and dimmed the lights. We didn't speak, not of Milo, or of Damon's bloodied knuckles, or of anything at all. We'd seen a helpless man murdered. There was nothing that could be said to make it better. His attackers were never found.

The last time I saw Damon lose his temper:

The morning of my funeral. Three days after I died, two days after our anniversary. The sun dared to shine, the world had the nerve to keep spinning. As Damon walked up the well—manicured walkway of the funeral home, he winced at the sound of birds singing. He turned a hard eye at the flowers, now all in their bloom. He grimaced at the sound of children laughing up the street. He swore under his breath at the smiling couple who passed him by.

"I'm burying my wife today, damn it," he said to no one, everyone.

He pulled open the door a little too hard, it was lighter than he'd anticipated. Immediately, the scent of baby powder and old lady perfume hit him. The director of Hannaford & Munson Funeral Home stood with his hand folded in front of him. When Damon's eyes landed on him, he nodded and smiled. Damon did not smile back. Instead, his wide glassy eyes darted around the parlor room. Velvet maroon curtains trimmed in gold. Floral armchairs and rows of folding chairs. A maroon settee. Flowers. So many flowers. He looked out the window. Then at his shaking hands. Anywhere but on the well—practiced sympathetic face of the parlor's director.

His chest rose and fell quickly, and a sheen of perspiration covered his forehead. The director approached. His bony hand on Damon's shoulder was enough to cause his jaw to clench, his teeth to grit. His body went rigid under the hand, but the man squeezed harder.

Abruptly, he stepped out from the well-intended grip and marched across the street and into the bakery across from the funeral home. In what was, for him, a most surreal moment, he ordered a coffee at the counter.

"Coffee, black."

"Good morning! What a great day to be alive, amiright?"

Damon looked around, as if unsure of where he was, or how he got there. He frowned and shook his head from side to side. Then he looked up and blinked at the cheerful barista, a man with a Gomer Pyle aww shucks face and toothy grin. His eyes widened at the man. He let out a hard, bitter sounding laugh, tilted his head and hissed,

"*What* did you say?"

The man faltered, his eyes taking in the telltale mourning suit. The man's smile shrunk, and he gave a small shrug, and in a smaller voice said,

"It's, uh, a great day to..."

With a suddenness that made the woman beside him gasp, Damon sprang forward. He grabbed fistfuls of the poor man's shirt in both hands and yanked him halfway over the counter.

"*Fuck* you. And fuck your good morning."

He shoved the stunned man back and became aware of the gasps and stares from the other patrons and workers.

"Sorry. Just — here."

Damon threw a twenty-dollar bill on the counter and left without his coffee. He trudged back across the street to the funeral home, oblivious of the traffic. His hands now shoved into his pockets as if he were afraid to set them free for fear of what they'd do next.

Five years, three displays of temper. All justified. Me? Please. I threw a fit when my toast was too dark, or my hair didn't turn out right. I smashed a vase once because I lost thirteen pages of a manuscript when my laptop failed. I was temperamental and irrational, especially in comparison to Damon. His goodness and thoughtful nature caused me to try to be better, in every single way.

So, for us, but mostly for him, I will figure this out. I must decipher the riddle of our paradox, give him the *why*. I ask the universe all the questions I was too obliviously happy to ask when I was alive.

Are we being punished? I've wondered it so many times since I've been dead. But today, I wonder: are we being given a kindness on this bleak February day? Maybe it's both. This is what I decide at *this* moment. It is both. The great yin and yang of the universe, the quintessence of karma. There is no light without darkness, no joy without pain, no peace without war. No love without... grief.

Maybe it's as simple as Newton's Third Law: For every action, there is an opposite but equal reaction. No meting out of judgment, no reward or punishment, there's just action, reaction. I'm not sure how I feel about this, other than frustrated. I don't even know if that's even in the ballpark of rightness. I'm just making wild guesses in the dark. There's still no one to ask.

But there is, Birdie, says the little voice in the back of my mind. The boy. *Damn it.*

"Babe?"

Damon shifts beside me, lifting his head even with mine and looking into my eyes. He blinks once, a slow sweep of dark lashes against his cheeks, and then his eyes searching mine. *Those eyes*. Oh, how I love his eyes. The color of roasted chestnuts. How many times have I lost my train of thought, or fell deeper in love, staring into those eyes? Countless. I do so now, as I struggle to tell him what will cause him more pain and possibly end this interlude.

There's a change in those eyes I love and know so well; a dilation of pupils. His body tenses against mine. He raises a finger to my lips, willing me to stop, but I must say it. So, I take his hand in mine and press it to my cheek and nudge my body even more against his.

"We need to go back," I whisper. "We have to go back to the island."

I hold my breath and wait for the sudden void of existence. It doesn't come. I am still here.

"To the island? Why?"

"I — I'm not exactly sure. There was... a boy. On the cliff."

At the mention of the cliff, Damon winces as if slapped. I place my hand on his warm cheek, slip my fingers through his soft hair and gaze into his eyes.

"I have to try and find him. I'm sorry."

"I didn't see — there was no boy. Not that I could see. Are you saying he was, I don't know, like an angel, or something?"

"I think so. Maybe?"

"Yeah? I'd like to get ahold of him myself, if so."

"Will you... can we go? I think it has to be on the anniversary of my..."

"Yes, yes. We'll go, Birdie. If it's what you want, or what you need, we'll go."

Damon sighs as he turns onto his back, keeping my hand clasped in his, against his heart. His eyes study the ceiling as if there might be answers there.

"I'm sorry, babe. I don't know what will happen, but I know it's important."

"Hey," he says, a soft smile turning up the corners of his mouth.

"Hmm?"

"You're still here, Birdie."

I smile, too.

TWELVE
<u>REAL</u>

I always seem to forget
How fragile are the very strong
I'm sorry I can't steal you
I'm sorry I can't stay
—A Bird's Song, Ingrid Michaelson

The time hops have stopped. So far, at least. Damon's birthday came and went, as did the remains of February and all of March. I'm still here...*ish*. Damon is the only one who sees me, it makes us both fear for his sanity. What if I am a figment of his wishful imagination? What if grief and solitude have driven him mad? He says, when I worry this aloud, that if so, it is the sweetest madness any man could ask for. I am not appeased.

When my mother arrives for her weekly visit, I stalk their interaction in hopes of gleaming a different perspective. Does he seem unwell to her? Does she eye him critically when he's not looking? Ultimately, Claire disproves and lessens my concern.

"Damon, I must say, you are looking so much better lately."

"Thank you, Claire. I — I'm feeling better."

My mother looks poised and elegant as ever, but with a strain to her eyes, that never used to be. She has her arms crossed in front of her. One finger tapping her chin, and she takes in his appearance with the eye of a fashion designer. Her nude-beige lipsticked lips part to say something, then close again with a slight smile and nod.

I know my mother well, I know what she's wondering. She wants to know if he's seeing someone, but she also does *not* want to know. If he moves on, falls in love again, she thinks she will lose her son-in-law.

"Good," she says instead.

"Coffee?"

"Yes, thank you. So, what have you been doing with yourself?"

"Oh, you know. The usual, work, uh, working out, the beach…"

Damon trails off. Claire tilts her head, drawing her delicate brows together at him for a brief moment. Then straightening herself, she changes the subject.

"Thomas and I are going on a cruise to Alaska next month. Isn't that crazy? It's supposed to be an amazing trip. The Hoffman's— you remember our neighbors, Max and Jane Hoffman? Well, they went last year and raved about it. So, we figured, why not?"

"Claire?"

"Yes, Damon?"

"I'm not seeing anyone. Just so you know."

Claire swallows hard, fidgets with her necklace. I want to cry for her. Instead of responding to what he's said, she tells him,

"I — I try. I just — every day, I try so hard to *be okay*."

Pulling a handkerchief from her purse, and pressing it gently under both eyes and just below her nose, Claire looks out past Damon. She gives a short head nod and continues as if she'll lose courage otherwise.

"I cry every day. Alone, of course. Tenley women... well, you know how we are. I will always be in mourning, Damon."

"And how is Thomas, Claire," Damon asks softly.

"Thomas? Ah, well. You know him. Bless his heart. I keep him fed and occupied. I signed us up for Round Robins at the tennis club, did I tell you? Took some pushing, but he's come around. Not moping about the house as much."

"What have you been doing for *you*, though?"

"Me? No need to worry about me, dear." Seeing his raised eyebrows, "I'm serious. I joined a book club. *And* volunteer as a baby snuggler in the NICU at St. Joseph's. I am fine, thank you very much. Now, back to you. You should. Start seeing someone, that is."

"Thank you, Claire, but I'm not interested in seeing anyone."

"Well, then. You will, dear. When the time is right for you, you will. Taylor would..."

"Here's your coffee. Let's sit out on the deck, it's warm today."

She follows him out through the French doors, sentences unfinished. When she leaves, a few hours later, Damon's face is ashen, his steps slow and heavy. The duplicity is wearing him out.

"I just wish I — *we* could give her some reprieve. You know, get her to see you like I do."

"I know. We've tried, though. Several times, and not just with her. Poor Aiden, he tries so hard. You're not going to let him bring that fake psychic back here again, are you? She went through the bathroom cabinet, you know."

"No, Madam Shania..."

"Sheila."

"...is not welcome again. I think she took our wine opener, too."

"The one with the lobster on top? No, I tossed it a while ago."

"What? I had no idea. I loved that thing."

"It was ridiculous. Had to go."

"I bought that for you when we were in Maine! You said you loved it."

"Didn't want to hurt your feelings," I shrugged and followed him to the kitchen.

It's like everything is normal, but of course, it's far from normal, this facsimile of life. But we pretend anyway. I lean on the cool, marbled grey granite kitchen island as Damon sets the coffee cups in the sink. His shoulder blades moving beneath the thin fabric of his t-shirt as he hand washes the cups and spoons are mesmerizing. His cell phone buzzes hard against the granite. We both jump.

I'm on the opposite side but can see the caller ID display. It's Doug. Again. I look up at Damon, his face is impassive. My stare is heavy on the crown of his head, and sensing it, he looks up, and his eyes meet mine with a warning glint.

I've tried several times to broach the subject, to no avail. Damon shuts down all discussion of Doug. He won't answer his calls, texts, or emails.

"What if he shows up one day? Then what?" I threw my hands in the air.

"He won't."

Damon is a master of compartmentalization. Everything, every feeling, every memory has its own box. Some, like his parents, stay locked with the keys thrown away. Others are open and closed often. Still others, like Milo's murder and my death, are allowed only brief exposures to light. Then closed as quickly as possible.

The Doug compartment is like a reverse fire safe. It doesn't protect the *contents* from fire damage so much as lock an inferno inside it.

I say nothing as the phone shimmies across the countertop, but my eyebrows remain raised. Damon ignores this *and* the call. Instead, he says,

"So, I booked our hotel. We're going to the damn island. I thought we'd drive to the port, then take a boat out ourselves. Like last time."

I half nod, now less sure of the plan now that it was becoming a reality. What if I'm wrong? Worse, what if I'm right? If the boy has the answers, *then* what happens? Do I disappear for good? The thought makes my stomach drop.

"Okay, great," I say, my voice sounding weak even to my own ears.

"Are you having second thoughts? We don't have to..."

"I think we do," I whisper.

Damon, looking down, gives a quick jerk of his head as he silences his phone. When his gaze finally meets mine again, it is with a grim acceptance. Our strange limbo has become safe, even if its security is probably false. Neither of us is ready to upset the peaceful balance anymore that we are willing to question it. At least not out loud.

The days are drifting lazily. We have been blissfully isolated from the world for much of the winter and early spring. But the seasonal residents will be returning, the stillness of the beach corrupted. It is becoming time to share Damon again with the world, and I am jealous. Yet, I'm not so jealous that I don't do and say the right things.

"Babe, I know your annual baseball trip is coming up. You should really go to the game with Charlie and Jack. It's tradition."

"We'll see, Birdie."

"Oh, no, you're not pulling the 'we'll see' trick. You know I've *never* fallen for that, right?"

"What? It's not a trick. I'm just...undecided."

"Undecided, my ass. '*We'll see*' means — and has always meant — '*nope*.' So, what happened? Last week you sounded like you were going, now, not so much. Spill it, Harrison."

Damon does the humming thing he does when avoiding a question. I wait. He caves.

"It's nothing, really. Charlie texted the other day and said they're bringing Linda and some woman Jack's been dating."

"But that leaves you, odd man... *oh*. They want to fix you up with someone."

"Yeah. Don't freak out, Birdie. I'm not going."

I sigh and let myself fall back into the couch cushions. It's so easy to forget when we're here, just the two of us. I'm dead, and Damon is alive. He is among the living, and it's where he belongs. Not holed up here with the paled version of his wife.

"You would've forced me, wouldn't you have?"

"What? Forced you to do what, Birdie?"

"If things were... reversed. If you were the ghost and I was the survivor, you'd have selflessly forced me to go live instead of keeping me hostage to a - a vision."

"A vision? Stop. You're not just a vision. You're real, and you're here. I don't know how or why, but this *is* real. You are real, you hear me? And you give me too much credit. If things were reversed, if I could still find you and be with you even after death, I would. So, enough of your worrying, okay? I'll say it again and again until you hear it: Let's take what we're given for as *long* as it's given."

Damon sits down beside me and pulls me to him. I nodded against his chest and wrap my arms around his waist. Deep down, though, I know I'll have to give him back to the world. When I find the boy.

THIRTEEN
QUESTIONS

*Mirror don't match the pictures on your wall
Yeah you've seen better days /You're not that man in a
frame / Young and proud and standing tall / It's a great
big world we've been living / Ain't so small what we've
been given, friend*
—Long Way to Go, The Lone Bellow

After much debate, Damon has gone to the game with Charlie, Jack, and…their *dates*. I stay behind, at home. I'm okay with this. I repeat it several times to no one.

"I'm totally okay. No big deal. Absolutely okay."

If someone could see me, they'd judge that my aimless pacing and arms crossed over my chest, tells otherwise. Then again, if someone (anyone besides Damon, that is) could see me, it'd mean I'm not dead. I guess.

By noon, I've tired of pacing the living room, and decide a walk along the beach is the perfect remedy for my restlessness. The sun is out, high in the clear blue sky and dancing like millions of fairies on the water. A perfect day but for my dark and depressing thoughts.

It's April, and there's only a handful of beachgoers on the beige sand. Joggers' sneakers pound the packed sand close to the shore. A couple of solitary readers sit with books and blankets further back. A man tosses a stick into the water for his yellow Labrador to retrieve.

I recognize him to be one of our neighbors, but can't recall his name. I do, however, remember the dog's name. Alfred. I don't know what possessed me, but I call out to him.

"Hey Alfred, old boy!"

Not expecting a reaction, of course. But Alfred *does* react. He stops midstride and drops his soggy stick onto the sand and looks in my direction. Correction: Alfred looks right at me. His tail wags stops, then wags again.

"Hey, buddy! You see me, huh? You're a good boy, Alfred."

This is all the encouragement Alfred needs. He trots with his big barrel body swaying cheerily over to me. His human — Bob, maybe... or Rob — looks on with his head cocked brow knitted.

"Hiya, pup," I say through unexpected tears.

The dog does that excited sit, stand, sit thing, his tail swishing in anticipation of being pet. I try. I run my hand over his silky dome and down his wet back, but he can't feel it. He whines and jaws, wiggling his fat bottom on the sand.

"You know I'm here, huh, Alfred? I'm frustrated, too, buddy."

Alfred's person takes several steps towards the dog but stops short. Perhaps he's deciding the dog should come to *him*, and not the other way around.

"Alfred!" He slaps his hand on his leg. "What are you *doing*, boy? Come!"

The pup acknowledges him with a half-turn and a rapid sweep of his tail but stays put. Bob (or Rob) gives a loud *tsk* sound and marches over to his weird acting dog and hooks a leash to Alfred's collar. Once the lead is secured, he looks up at me. No, *through* me, around the immediate vicinity, and back down at his dog who is again whining in hopeful agitation. I watch them walk away, each turning back several times over their shoulders, then decide I'm over taking a walk.

As I approach the house, movement from inside catches my eye.

Damon has come home early!

But the person sitting on the couch in the living room, his back to the French doors, does not have Damon's dark curls. Or his build. My heart stutters in my chest, an icy chill pricks my skin.

The slicked back hair, the watch gleaming on the casual arm slung across the couch back. It's Doug.

As fast as the fear struck, comes a hot fury, replacing the stutter with a pounding. My temples pulse and my teeth grit as I steel myself for the sight of his face.

Calm down, Birdie. He can't do anything to you ever again.

"Hello, you piece of shit," I say aloud.

There is pure venom in my voice, it shakes with it. Nothing. He checks the time on his watch, then rests his arm on the sofa's back again and looks around. He has one leg crossed over the other, argyle—socked ankle resting on his knee.

"Mr. Fucking Casual, huh? Making yourself comfortable, are you?"

There are beads of sweat at his temple. His long leg bounces and his foot taps on the hardwood floor. All the while, his manicured fingers drum the backrest.

"Hmm. Maybe you're not so comfortable, are you? Do you know that Damon knows? Is that why you're so nervous?"

He slicks back his already slicked hair. More white streaks are weaving through the blond than last year. His cold slate eyes cut to the mantle, and land on the picture of Damon and I dancing to I Can't Give You Anything but Love, Baby. Looks away with a quick jerk. Is that guilt I see? *Good.*

"You *should* feel guilty, you asshole."

Doug pulls out his phone, starts to tap keys on the pad, then tosses it aside. It bounces once on the sofa cushion. He stands instead, leaving the phone on the sofa and paces the living room floor, then walks into the kitchen. I follow his every move, willing my body to take form, be seen. Next, he pulls open the refrigerator door and takes one of my husband's beers. Opens our drawers one by one until he finds an opener.

STILL HERE

The raging fire in my chest is growing, spreading up my neck and through my scalp. His every breath, every invasive touch of our belongings is another violation.

He tips his head back along with the bottle and takes a long sip. My eyes narrow as his Adam's apple bobs with each swallow. His neck is stubbled, he hasn't shaved in a couple days. His button-down shirt is wrinkled and untucked. His grey-blue eyes are bloodshot. Something has happened in Doug's universe. But what?

"What did you do now, Doug? Has Melissa figured out who you are, *what* you are?"

I don't expect an answer, nor do I get one. He finishes the beer, sets the bottle down without looking. The bottle totters and falls over with a sharp clink. It rolls down the counter like a bowling ball, then falls to the floor. He makes no move to stop it. It lands with a hollow plunk but doesn't shatter. Doug saunters around the counter, once. Twice. He ignores the bottle.

These aren't the actions of a *nervous* man. This is the behavior of a man wrestling with barely contained agitation. *Anger.* I recognize it well, I am following him in much the same way. Now my eyes slant at his back.

"What are you doing here, Doug?"

Instead of returning to the living room, he heads towards the stairs, pausing only briefly before taking them two at a time. He strides straight to our bedroom and doesn't even have the decency to hesitate before he walks in. The bed is unmade, both pillows askew. My clothes still hang in the closet. My vanity still enshrines my perfumes and make—up, brush and jewelry box.

The bed is the first thing he homes in on. He gives a derisive sniff and shakes his head.

"Still hanging on, huh? Jesus, Damon."

I jump at his voice even as I realize he's only talking aloud, to no one. There's contempt in his tone, not sympathy, and it causes the hairs on the back of my neck to stand. Doug turns his attention to my vanity and lifts my perfume bottle to his nose. He throws his head back and breathes in the honey—citrus scent. His eyes closed, his hand moves to the front of his pants, and he squeezes himself through the denim. My stomach lurches and my throat constricts as I watch him, but I can't look away. I can see his erection straining against the material.

"You *fucking pig*," I shout.

The perfume bottle drops from his hand, and he whips around.

"Who's there?"

I open my mouth to answer, then close it again. I'll let him convince himself that he only heard the wind, and nothing more. For now. He replaces the bottle on the vanity and moves across the room to my closet, where he begins to paw my dresses and blouses. He stops at a sheer nightgown and runs his fingers over where my breast would be.

"You son of a bitch."

From the doorway, I sprang and rush across the room, white-knuckled fists at my sides. I get between him and my nightgown, but his lecherous hand drops down, and his cold eyes stare through me. He is calm and oblivious to how close I am to him, but my face burns crimson hot, and my hands are shaking.

He turns his back on the closet, on me, and makes his way over to the dressers where the row of photographs sit. All the ones with him in them are gone, but there is still one of Damon, Melissa, and I posing ridiculously for the camera.

He studies it for several minutes. Then he takes it down and taps the glass, hard, right where Damon's smiling face is.

"Always the fucking hero, right buddy? Mr. Do-No-Wrong Damon *fucking* Harrison. Everybody loves ya, man. Forever the martyr. Lose your parents, aww *poor Damon*. Lose your wife, *poor Damon*. Men want to be you, ladies want to fuck you."

He glances around conspiratorially as if he and his cronies were shaking down a lowly shopkeeper for protection money. Then, in a needling tone,

"Did you fuck my wife, buddy? You must've, man. Just fucking admit it. You fucked my wife, and *I* almost fucked *yours*. But almost doesn't... *fucking*...count."

He sniffs and shrugs, collecting himself in front of his invisible audience. Then he peers hard at the photograph again.

"Whatever, man, whatever. All I know is, after yours and *Birdie's* visit last summer, she wouldn't let me touch her, let alone fuck her. So, I really wanna know, my friend, what the fuck happened in my house."

I'm sickened by what I'm seeing and hearing from his vile mouth. He has no remorse, no guilt.

"You're a Goddamn sociopath," I sputter at him.

Is *this* the real Doug Miller? Was the other Doug— the one Damon has known for nearly twenty years— a facade? My gut clenches as images of that awful night replay in my head, the morning after. Mel. Her question.

"Hey, did you— did happen to see Doug at all last night? Like, during the night, I mean."

My lie. Could she have read something in my tone, or seen something in my eyes? Did she know, or did something else happen? I back away from Doug and sit heavily on the edge of the bed, my hands to my face.

"My God, have you done this before? Again?"

Tears prick my eyes...*perhaps my silence has cost another woman her security.* Downstairs, the sound of the front door opening.

Doug sets down the picture frame, does a quick double take at the still unpatched holes in the wall, and saunters calmly out the bedroom door. I rush past him, towards the stairs. From below,

"Babe? I'm ho..."

"Damon..."

Before I can tell him, *Doug is in the house*—

"Well, hey there, *babe*."

Damon freezes, his eyes scan my face, then shift to Doug.

"Doug."

"You've been avoiding me, man."

He took each stair like a gunslinger, says the next words in time with each step.

"And I...want...to know...why."

Damon, his body tensed like a lion ready to pounce, sets down his keys. He pulls his phone from his pocket and places it down as well. He takes off his faded baseball cap and rakes his hair back. All just as slowly as Doug has taken the stairs. But he doesn't answer yet. I can see his jaw clenching and unclenching. His nostrils flare. Doug looks unperturbed by Damon's silence.

"So, who '*babe*'? You got yourself a new woman, huh? Didn't take you long. Not that I thought it would. Mr. Amazing, never a shortage of adoring women lining up to comfort the poor widower, right?"

Doug smiles that smile of his, the one that never reaches his eyes, and spreads his arms wide, as if ready to receive a hug. Our floor plan is open, the foyer opens into the wide living room on the left, and the kitchen to the right. Doug walks to the left and casually treads over to the mantle, placing himself only the sofa's length away from Damon. If Doug is aware of the simmering hate in Damon's eyes, he shows no acknowledgment and has the nerve to continue.

"I guess I'm just full of questions today, aren't I, old pal? You know what I'm *most* curious about, though? I'm curious if *you*, my lovelorn friend, are getting *comforted* by *my* wife. Because you two... well, you two have always had a special little something. So, tell me, Damon. Are you fucking my wife?"

Damon had been watching his every move stonily. At these words, though, his eyes widen, then he scoffs, shaking his head. He takes steady, slow steps towards Doug. They are the same height, equal opposites in every way. Where Damon is lean and muscular like a thoroughbred, Doug is stocky and solid like a mule. A physical fight between them would depend on whose fury was greater. I try to caution Damon.

"Babe, he's not worth it. He's out of his mind. Please, just get him out of here, okay?"

I know that Damon hears me, I see the flicker in his eyes, the slight tilt of his head in my direction, but he ignores my plea. He takes another step towards Doug. At last, he speaks.

"That's what you're most curious about? See, that's funny, *old pal*. Here I am, thinking that maybe, just maybe, you came here to ask my forgiveness."

"Forgiveness?"

Doug tries to say it with a sneer, but a flicker of fear passes through his eyes.

"Forgiveness. You know, for trying to rape my wife, you son of a bitch."

Damon's hands are fisted, but he maintains his self—control.

"Rape? Is that what she called it? Please. She came out to that barn in just a t-shirt. Sorry to disillusion you about your precious *Birdie*, but she *wanted* it, Dam—"

Damon's fist connects with Doug's cheekbone before the sentence is finished. He's knocked backward by the blow and grabs the mantle to keep from falling, knocking the photograph to the floor.

Damon looks away from Doug to the falling frame and Doug uses the distraction to charge him.

The men crash to the floor, Damon's head barely missing the edge of the coffee table. They are a furious tangle of fists and grunts, throwing an equal number of sickening blows. There's blood on the carpet, the seat of the sofa, their clothes, and faces, but they don't stop.

Damon has somehow gotten on top of Doug and is landing bone breaking punches to his face. He's going to kill him.

He's going to kill him.

"Damon! Stop," I yell.

His fist pauses in midair, and he looks up at my horror-stricken expression, then back down at Doug's bloody face. His hands are up defensively to ward off the next blow, and his one good eye has widened in shock. He heard my voice.

Damon climbs off him in disgust, grabbing the front of Doug's shirt and pulling him up roughly as he does. When they are both shakily standing, Damon shoves him back hard enough to make him stumble. Giving him no time to recover his balance, Damon shoves him again.

Doug is too shocked to retaliate but looks back and forth from Damon to me. *He can see me.* And, yes, he looks as though he's seen a ghost.

"*Get out.* Get the fuck out of our house, and don't ever come back. You understand me?"

"I— she…this is impossible. You're…"

"Do not fucking speak to her. Look at me, Doug. If you ever come near us again, I will kill you. You hear me? I will kill you."

Doug is barely processing what his eyes are showing him, but he *does* hear Damon's threat and nods convulsively. His jacket and keys are on the chair by the door. He grabs them without looking, feels behind him for the doorknob, and backs out the front door. Damon follows him to the doorway, his bloodied hands gripping the door and frame.

When Doug's engine revs and gravel spits out from the tires, Damon slams the door hard enough that the picture on the wall crashes to the floor. He doesn't turn around, so I come up behind him and rest my head against his back. He reaches back and finds my hand and pulls it around him, to his chest. Over his heart. It's beating hard and fast, but we stay like this until it slows and steadies.

This time, he leads me upstairs to our bathroom. We bypass the ransacked living room without sparing it a glance. We'll deal with it later. I turn the shower faucets on full blast, let the steam fill the room. He complies obediently as I grip the hem of his stained and torn shirt, pull it from his arms and over his bowed head. He has yet to look at me, my gaze has not left him.

He kicks off his shoes. I unbutton his pants, lower the zipper and slip my hands into the waistband. Then I slide his boxers and pants down his muscled thighs to the floor. He steps out of them and lets me walk him to the shower. The pale pink slip that I've taken to wearing falls to the floor and I step into the stream of water with him.

As the hot water rains down over us, I wrap my arms around his naked body, close my eyes, and rest my chin against his chest. Damon bends his head to mine and kisses my forehead.

"Birdie…"

"Shhh," I tell him, "I know. I know."

He turns around, lets me wash his hair, leaning back against my hands, and we say nothing more. We switch positions, and I lather soap across his chest, down his arms, and over his buttocks and the hardness pressed against my belly. He winces when the soap seeps into his cuts but says nothing.

I am cleaning away more than the physical reminders of what has just occurred, I am cleansing his soul. He doesn't have to tell me he feels the burden of guilt for not protecting me from Doug. Or that, had I not stopped him, he would've killed him. I know his thoughts as if they were my own. I always have. I know him by heart.

FOURTEEN
STAGES

Stars fading but I linger on dear
Still craving your kiss
I'm longing to linger till dawn dear
Just saying this
—Dream a Little Dream, Ella Fitzgerald

Time, in its traditional sense, has continued. I am still here. It's become increasingly difficult for Damon to explain his isolation to those who know and love him. People have expectations of how grieving should work. It has stages, as you know.

For example, at year marker one— which we are breathing down the neck of— Damon is expected to be at the *acceptance* stage. Of course, no one will come out and say that. But it's implied.

Aiden:

"So, Damon," began Aiden last week, "how are we doing? Are we…getting back out there? Are we seeing anyone?"

Claire:

"Well, now, Damon. Aren't you looking handsome and refreshed! You're just about ready to start your next chapter, I can tell."

Thomas:

"Hey, son. How about we take a guy's fishing trip? Like the old days!"

Jack and Charlie are much the same. Even his editor has chimed in with suggestions. Everyone is ready for him to *get on with life*. Damon gives them noncommittal shrugs and nods, thanks them for their continued support. Even to his own ears, he sounds like a politician playing to his constituents.

My name is now a word infrequently spoken, surreptitiously, or after too much wine. Thinking back to when I was alive, I realize I did this as well, treating the dead as if they were…gone. Sure, the dead get pulled from their slumber on holidays and birthday, anniversaries of death and so on. Dust off the memories, visit the grave, shed some tears. But the business of life goes otherwise on.

I'm sorry. I'm melancholy today. My thoughts are bitter and mean. I know I'm not forgotten, but I want to hear them say my *name*. I want them to know I'm here, sitting beside them or walking about the room. I want to feel my mother's arms around me, I want to hear my father call me Peach. I want Aiden to call me a skinny bitch. I want my life back, damn it.

"Birdie? I'm almost packed. We'll leave in an hour, okay?"

Oh, and then there's that. Our trip back to the place where…to the island. I thought I'd be more excited, more *ready*. But I'm not. I'm nowhere near ready to say goodbye to Damon. My brain is pleading, *no, let's just stay here.*

"Sure, babe. I'm ready when you are."

He watches me a moment longer, his eyes solemn and round, unspoken words hovering on his lips. He swallows them hard and walks back to the bedroom. I stay on the balcony, watching the waves dance in the moonlight as if it's the last time I'll ever see it. Then I join him in the bedroom, sit on the bed and watch him pull clothes from drawers.

"Babe?"

Damon turns only his head, giving me his profile. His long lashes rest against his cheek, his body still and waiting. He is a man in pause.

"Come sit with me. Please."

He hangs the shirt over the drawer, not bothering to return it or pack it, takes a weighted breath and comes to me. He doesn't sit beside me but instead goes to his knees before me, between my legs, head in my lap. Like a lost boy, my love. I slip one hand through his thick hair and the other under the collar of his shirt, between his shoulder blades, against his hot skin. *We* are on pause.

Into the thin material of my dress, against my thigh, he says...

"What if..."

I wait.

"What if I can't see or hear you, but you're still here?"

I have no answer.

"What if you don't find the boy?"

I look down at the silky locks of his hair curling around my fingers and sigh. I've thought the same thoughts, asked the same questions and more, but have yet to know the answers. Perhaps they aren't for us to know. I can only counter his questions with my own.

"What if I'm still here, just like this, after the island?"

He tightens his grip on my hips.

"What if I *do* find the boy, and he has no answers?"

The last question is the hardest, but I ask anyway.

"What if... what if this is all a long goodbye?"

Damon looks up then, shakes his head. Denial? Refusal? He says,

"What if you get to stay? What if *nothing*, not even death can keep us apart? What if you are mine, and I am yours forever?"

He says this with force and determination as if he can *will* the universe into making it so. There is no response I can give him, so instead, I take his sweet face in my hands and kiss his mouth softly. The love I feel for him is wider and deeper than the ocean outside our doors.

Damon lowers his head back into my lap again, pushes the smooth fabric of my dress up higher, and places a trail of soft kisses up my thighs. His tongue flicks at my center, and all thoughts are banished. We make the kind of slow, soul-shaking love that two people make when they know there's no tomorrow.

Afterwards, we close the house and load his duffel bag into the Jeep. The night is warm, and we drive with the top off, racing against the moon and stars high above us. I let my arm rest on the window frame and watch my hand roll against the rushing wind. I spread my fingers wide and feel the air slip through. *My life has slipped through my fingers.* The thought comes unbidden, unwelcome.

The melancholy has enshrouded us like a fog. The brightness of the moon and stars are in stark contrast. I lay my cheek on my outstretched arm and let the wind blow my hair all around. At a stoplight, Damon brushes the wind tossed strands from my face, I take his hand in mine and kiss his palm.

The Jeep moves us through the night, and the world around us is nothing more than a blur of colors and nondescript images. They are the ones moving fast while we go in slow motion, towards our dreaded destination. Wishful thinking, I suppose.

Slow down, I want to say. *Stop*, is on the tip of my tongue, tasting like lead and panic. The words won't come. So, I shift in my seat and face Damon so I can watch his profile illuminate ghostly white under the streetlamps as we pass below them. He feels my gaze and turns to me, his eyes shining. His jaw works, he is willing himself to be strong. *I don't want to do this*, his eyes plead.

I want to give in, say *okay, forget it, we don't have to, babe*. But I'm reminded of when I had to put Maximillian down. I gave Damon the same look, that desperate beg, that '*I can't,*' even though I knew I could and I must. When *I* faltered at what must be done, Damon poured all his strength into me so I will do the same for him. For us.

STILL HERE

The harsh lights of the toll booth pull us from our solitary confinement and Damon is forced to speak.

"Good evening, that's one dollar, sir."

"Here you go."

His voice is like a rusty hinge.

"You're all set. You two have a lovely night."

We both give a start. *You two.*

"Excuse me, you... you can see my wife?"

"Son, I may be old, but I am not blind. 'Specially when there's a lovely lady around."

He emphasizes with a wink in my direction. Damon guides the Jeep back into a lane. We're both confused. Sure, there's been those few moments. But... this. This is new. What could it mean? What if... and here we are again with what ifs.

"Your parent's exit is next."

"You think we should..."

Damon nods. I'm unsure, fearful. What if...what if...what if? There's so many of them to choose from. Damon answers my unasked questions with...

"What if they *can* see you? What if it *is* permanent? What if," his voice breaks, "what if you're being given a chance to say goodb..."

The word drops off, swallowed by night. I nod, once. Damon takes the exit, its sharp curve that always meant *almost home*. I exhale each breath slowly through my mouth, forcing the butterflies to quell. To hug them once more... I don't dare to hope.

The windows of the old cornflower-blue colonial are dark, and for a moment I think, *they're not home*. But then there's the flicker of the television through the window and the silhouette of two people on the sofa sitting close together. Damon kills the lights as he pulls into the drive, but before he can get out of the car, I stop him.

"Wait." I breathe the word out.

I'm suddenly unsure. Is this cruel? I want to watch them a few moments more before I tell Damon my decision. A smile pulls at my lips as they laugh in unison at the screen. Comedies. My mother will only watch comedies. *Real life is full of enough drama*, she always says. My father indulges her even though he only likes documentaries on war. Or shows about how things are built.

My death has brought them closer, I realize. The event well known for tearing couples and families apart has strengthened their bond. I'm moved, gladdened, and yes, saddened. My place in their life is their past. I could only bring them pain. So, when Damon puts his hand on the door handle again, I stop him.

"Babe...don't. I don't want to... I can't put them through it again."

He considers whether to argue with me, then watches my parents through their window for a few moments. Then he nods.

"Okay."

The engine purrs to life again, and we roll back out. Just as the back tires touched the street, the front door opens, and light spills out from the foyer. Claire has one hand on the door frame, the other waving. Damon looks to me for what to do, but I am a deer in headlights, frozen.

"Damon?" she called out.

STILL HERE

He gives her a short wave and pulls back into the driveway. There is no turning back now. What will be, will be.

"I knew that was you!" she calls behind her, "I told you it was Damon in the drive, Thomas. Now, what are you doing out here so— oh! You have someone with you."

To her credit, she sounds merely surprised. But her surprise is about to be more than mere, it will be shock.

"Damon, you have to prepare her somehow. Go, quick."

Damon is catapulted into action and jumps out the car before Claire can approach. My face is hidden by the shadows.

"Claire, hey! Sorry to show up unannounced and so late. I— uh, you're going to want to sit down Claire."

My father has now joined them, looking surprised and concerned, but pleased.

"Tom, you too."

"Damon, sweetheart, invite your friend in, too!"

"We'll get to that. I need you to do something for me, and it's kind of an impossible request."

He glances back in my direction.

"Buddy, you're starting to make me nervous, here," laughs my father.

My mother likely thinks she is being prepared to meet a new girlfriend. I can tell she is arranging her expression to look warm and receptive, even though she feels anything but. This was the face she wore for every boy I ever brought home before Damon.

"Hush, Thomas. Damon, what is this impossible request?"

"I, well, I need you to, uh, suspend your disbelief."

They slow blink at him, then each other.

"Hear me out, okay? What if... what if I told you that Birdie was here. Like, somehow, *here*. Right now?"

Their demeanor changes again. Now it is that of parents readying themselves to placate and comfort a child who's claimed to have seen the Boogeyman in his closet.

"Oh, honey," my mother begins, "you poor thing. I understand. Tomorrow is the anniversary of her... *and* your wedding anniversary. I'm so sorry I didn't reach out today. I should've known you'd be..."

"No, Claire. I mean, yes, that. But, I don't know how, or why, but Birdie's... ghost or whatever, and now she's... but I don't know how long she'll... damn it. This is coming out all wrong."

He turns back to the jeep, throws his hands up and shakes his head. Then he says one word, like a plea for help.

"Birdie?"

I hesitate a moment, then open my door and walk around the back of the Jeep. I am not yet in the light, they cannot fully see me, but I hear my mother gasp. A mother knows her child's gait, profile, mannerisms; she knows her child anywhere. One step more will take me into the light. No turning back.

"How..." my mother whispers.

"Peach...?" my father chokes.

Damon keeps a hand on my mother's arm, keeping her steady, and his eyes on me. I tuck my hair behind my ear, and this is Claire's undoing.

"Oh," she sighs, a hand to her chest, another to her mouth, "my baby. My baby... but how? How is this..."

She's taking slow, unsure steps across the driveway to me, I am momentarily frozen in place. But then she spreads her arms wide and nods as if to say everything is alright, come to your mother. I say the only thing I can at this moment that shouldn't be.

"Mommy..."

I haven't called her that since I was eight. But in my heart, I am eight again, and I need my mother's comfort. I close the distance between us and fall into my mother's frail yet powerful arms.

"Oh, my sweet girl."

Her tone is incredulous, bewildered, and full of love. My poor father is still on the porch, uncomprehending. Damon brings him down to join us beside the Jeep. He stands slightly behind Damon, like a shy child meeting his teacher for the first time.

"Hi, Daddy."

"Peach? I don't— we don't understand. What's happening here?"

"Why don't you come inside," says my mother, ever the hostess, "we'll talk over coffee."

Damon and I exchange looks, I give a small head shake, he understands.

"Actually, we can't. I'm sorry," he begins, but I interrupt.

"Mom, Daddy, we don't really know what's happened— what's happening. But I *do* know I need to go back to the island, I have to be there tomorrow."

"No."

My mother says this forcefully, then again petulantly.

"*No.*"

"Peach, why? Why do you have to go back... there? I think, whatever's happened, however, it is you're here, we should just take it. No questions asked."

Damon wants to agree with my father, I can see him begin to nod in agreement. They want to see this as a hostage situation. One where they've told my captors that they don't want any trouble, just give us back the girl. But he sees the resolution in my face. As does my mother.

This isn't about what we want or need, it's about... well, I don't know what it's about. But if I were forced to give an opinion as to what I *think* this is, I guess I'd say: it is a lesson in presence. In *being*. Not looking for horizons and tomorrows, or back on yesterdays. It's about now. I tell them this as best I can. Since it came from a woman who is, by all accounts, dead and gone (but still here), they nod solemnly as if I hold the answers to the secrets of the universe. I don't say that I am guessing, that the words *feel* right. But I also pull no punches. If the shock of my post-death visit hasn't killed them, nothing I can say now will.

"I think I'm here to say goodbye. We won't know until…"

Until after tomorrow. Until after I find the boy. If I find the boy. But deep down, I know I will. Damon picks up where I leave off.

"We're driving to the port, then taking a boat out to the island. Birdie thinks that if she finds…"

I continue for him.

"There was a boy, just before I jumped — or fell, I guess it was. I need to see if he is there if he is an… angel. *My* angel, I think I mean. If there *are* any explanations to be found, he is the one I have to ask."

I don't add 'I think' again. Not aloud, at least. It's become redundant. My parents and Damon all nod as if this makes perfect sense. We've crossed so far over into the surreal, that there's no choice but to accept the impossible.

"Well, sweetheart," my mother begins, "if that is what you must do, that that is what you'll do."

"Claire," my father, though still bewildered, is about to argue, "no, she should stay put and…"

"Nonsense, Thomas. The only thing we should all do right now is have faith. That is what we're *going* to do, you hear?

We all nod obediently. Claire has spoken, it is as good as law. I so love this about my mother; her strength is indisputable, insurmountable, and unmatchable. What a role model I have been blessed with, both in life and after death.

I have so much to say to them. I thought that I was going to recite all the times they were the best parents a girl could have. How I always knew the depth of their love for me. That I was sorry for being such a bitch during the teen years. That I'm sorry, I confess: when I was nine, I flushed their tickets to a weekend music festival down the toilet because I was jealous they weren't taking me. That I've always loved Daddy's nickname for me. There were volumes of paragraphs of words for feelings welling up inside of me, and all I can say is,

"I love you guys. So much..." before the tears overcome me. Gone is my composure and philosophical musings. I'm just a girl saying goodbye to her mom and dad forever. I'm their baby, cocooned in their arms, our silent tears rolling down our stricken faces. My sweet Damon is standing back, with all his broken grace, giving us our precious time, and letting his own unchecked tears splash to the pavement.

My mother is the first to pull back. She gives Daddy's arm a pat, then takes my face in her thin, delicate hands. Her wedding ring is cold against my cheek. She searches my eyes, trying to absorb every pore, freckle, and line. She's making this moment, this gift and curse of goodbye, last her forever.

Daddy takes her place and pulls me none too gently into a bear hug. I breathe in the scent of his cologne, the only one he's ever worn, and it brings me back to every boo-boo made better, my first car accident, graduation, my wedding. Every hug Daddy's ever given, for every reason ever, is wrapped into *this* hug.

When he reluctantly let's go, Damon takes his place by my side, wraps my hand in his and squeezes reassuringly.

"I'm sorry," he begins to say to them.

"None of that, son. Thank you. I— *we*, we can't thank you enough," says Thomas.

Damon nods, visibly conflicted by their gratitude.

"I feel like I'm stealing your daughter away from you yet again."

Claire shakes her head, and ever the mom tells him,

"Damon, you have always been as much a gift to us as our girl, here. We love you, sweetheart. Whatever happens on that island... *we love you*."

They hug for a long moment. Daddy gives him the man hug, and then we climb back into the Jeep. As we pull out of the drive, I keep my eyes on them. Daddy has his arm protectively around my mother's slight shoulders. His big hand is clasped in both of her small ones, and her head leans against his broad chest. I turn to watch them, but all too soon, they are out of sight. I sigh and face forward again, and we continue onward.

FIFTEEN
SUNRISE

Sail away with me honey I put my heart in your hands
Sail away with me honey now, now, now
Sail away with me What will be will be
I wanna hold you now
—Sail Away, David Gray

We arrive at the dock before the sun has risen.

"Good morning! You two honeymooners?"

"What? Oh, uh, no. Just a... an overnight trip. Here's our reservation number."

"You two been here before? Ya look familiar. 'Specially you, Miss."

"Oh, I just have one of those faces, I guess."

The man eyed me a moment longer, that almost—dawning of recognition hovering in his eyes. Damon distracted him.

"Okay, so I paid online for the boat, I think all my info is here."

"Right, yup. Looks like you're all set. For another hundred bucks, we can charter the boat for you, and you two can relax and enjoy the ride."

"We're all set, thanks."

"Suit yourself, buddy."

I thank him again, and we board the rental boat. It's a three hour and forty-minute ride to the small island, we'll be making good time despite our unplanned stop. This time last year, we made this same trip. I wore this dress, and Damon wore that shirt, his baseball cap backward. My sunglasses on top of my head, holding my hair back from the wind.

On that day, we laughed and sang along to Damon's 'Sailing Playlist' and drank champagne with strawberries at the bottom of the glasses. We watched a pod of dolphins break the water in graceful arcs and waved to another couple as they sailed past us. It was a peaceful, magical day until...

Today, of course, is so terribly different. We're trying to recreate a memory whose edges are blackened and jagged. The beauty is tarnished by the ending. Everything from our clothes to the boat, to the ocean itself, are a cold slap and a mean reminder of what's lost. What's about to be lost again.

"Birdie?"

I look at Damon, standing at the helm like a cross between Jack Sparrow and Jacques Cousteau, and can't help but smile. Whatever he was about to say melts away, and he smiles back at me. We've made an unspoken agreement that for right now, and for as long as we can, we are going to be just us. Damon and Birdie, living.

I join him at the wheel. He puts his arms around me, and we sail off to whatever is waiting for us with as much grace and dignity as we can muster. The sun, heavy and tiger-orange, balances on the horizon and the water dances like liquid fire all around it. We watch its ascent, determined to absorb every ounce of beauty. Every moment must be captured and engraved in our memory. *Be in the moment* is the mantra in our minds.

Listen, I'd be lying if I said I'm not still thinking hopeful and horrible *what ifs*. They nag at the back of my mind like an unreachable itch. *Be in the moment*. But, what if…

Be in the moment.

Damon feels my restlessness, knows its source, and kisses the back of my head. It is his turn to be the pacifier, the philosophizer, the pragmatist to my quiet hysteria.

"It's just as we've said, we have been given extra time, and we don't know why, or how, or for how long. Maybe we'll never know why, or maybe everything will become clear. I don't know the answers to any of this either, but I know I'm grateful, Birdie. Whatever happens from here on out, I am so damn grateful."

Passion gives tremor to his voice. I nod against his chest.

"Me, too, babe."

Right now, this is enough. I'm able to let go of the questions and fears again, and yes, *be in the moment*. When you know that your time is limited, days numbered, everything becomes brighter, sharper, bolder. You work harder to see and feel. You try to absorb every detail, fill every moment with purpose. I can't help but imagine — cliché as it may sound — what life would be like if we all lived as if we were dying.

SIXTEEN
TUMAU

Come with me My love
To the sea The sea of love
—Sea of Love, Phil Phillips

We take a room in the same hotel, different room from the last time. That one had overlooked the cliffs and the ocean. This one does not.

"What now?" Damon asked.

I spread my arms wide, palms up, and shrug. There is no manual for us to follow, no guide or instructions. There is just us. It is fitting, though. From the moment we met, we've been on our own island, in our own world. Why *would* this be any different?

"I think… let's go have breakfast," I decide.

"Breakfast?"

"Yes. The meal before lunch."

Damon gives me 'the look.'

"Very funny. Glad you can still be a wiseass."

He smiles, though. I take his face in my hands, smiling against his lips. In a swift movement, he's wrapped his arms around my waist and lifted me off the floor and spun me onto the bed. Our lovemaking is hungry and fierce. We claim each other for eternity, *against* eternity.

Damon's head is bowed to my chest, his soft curls tickling my neck, his breath warm against my breast. His heart beats hard against my belly. *Oh, this love.* In this new moment I decide, '*Fine, I accept. If this is all I'm allowed for this lifetime, I accept.*' I give up my greed and selfish need for *more*. I give up all expectations. We have been blessed with great love. A love greater than I could have ever imagined possible. No one owed it to us, it wasn't an entitlement. It was a gift.

I want to say this to Damon, to help him be okay when this all ends. When I'm gone. He can sense my shift, knows I wish to say something, so he lifts his gaze to mine. My breath catches in my throat. My God, he is beautiful. His chestnut eyes and sun-kissed russet locks, his cheekbones, and lips, his strong chin. He is perfection to my imperfection. He is my fairy tale.

"It's alright, Birdie. I know. No matter what happens, we have been the fortunate ones, haven't we?"

I can only nod.

"I've always known it, Birdie. From the moment I first saw you, I knew. We've been together for a thousand lifetimes, and we'll be together for a million more. I'm *always* going to be with you. Just…trust me. That's all you have to do, okay?"

"I will. Always."

And this *is* our truth. Damon has always known it, and I've always just gone along, hopeful, but not confident. But I know it with his same certainty now. The weight and the worry, so like a storm cloud, has lifted. The sunlight streams in through the windows as much as it does my soul.

"Good. Let's go eat."

I laugh and shove him playfully off me. We dress and go into the village for coffee and breakfast, finding a table outside. When the waitress brings two menus, I sigh with relief. *I am still here.*

We look like any other couple on the island. Suntanned and in love, drinking coffee, and making plans for the day ahead. Only, the plans we make are not ones of fun and frolic. Although...

"Damon?"

"Mhmm," he responds, coffee cup against his lips.

"I think we should just relax and enjoy the day. Let's not— let's not make it..."

"Climatic?"

"Yes. Exactly. Let's take our own advice and..."

"Be in the moment."

We say it together. The waitress overhears the last part and smiles down at us. She is clad in a bright, colorful skirt, white blouse and teal scarf hold back her long dreadlocks. With a Jamaican lilt, she exclaims,

"Now, that's how to *live*! You two got the right idea. Honeymoon?"

"Anniversary," we say.

"Oh, well, happy anniversary, lovebirds! You enjoy your day, now."

We thanked her and wished her the same, then smiled at one another. Damon leans back in his chair and stretches his long legs, his ankle pressed against mine. We are tethered to each other. I breathe in deeply the briny air, taste the hazelnut coffee as it touches my tongue, and the warmth slips down my throat. Every sensation is heightened, now that we are in the moment. The smooth handle of my cup. The tiny particles of white sugar on the small black bistro table. A spot of coffee on my napkin. The hairs on Damon's leg against my smooth ankle. Every detail is sharp.

An elderly couple strolls down the street. Her arm, creped with age, is hooked through his, and he smiles down at her as she points towards the ocean. Damon watches me as I watch them. The stores are opening one by one and vendors hang scarves on overhead hooks and roll tables of souvenirs out front for passersby.

There is one spot I have not let my eyes travel to. The cliffs. They are only partially visible from my vantage point at the outdoor café. Bits of brown rock, fragments of aquamarine water sparkling in the sun. I have avoided looking in that direction, as has Damon since we arrived. Soon enough, we will look, and then take the winding drive up to the top, and we will see what is next.

"Shall we take a walk through the town?" asks Damon.

"Why yes, I think we shall."

Damon pays our tab and gives a wave to the friendly waitress as we leave, who in return gives us a wink and a huge smile. I hear her say to the young couple she's serving,

"Now, those two know how to live, mon."

The fresh-faced couple looks after us, smiles on their faces. Perhaps envisioning themselves several years down the road in our likeness, as I'd imagined when watching the elderly couple. Oh, to have the crystal ball vision of what the future holds. What might we do with it, I wonder? My eyes are drawn to the colorful silk scarves waving in the breeze, so I pull Damon over to the stall. It's silly, I know, to be engaging in such normal activities when I should be looking for the boy. But we're determined to make this last us as long as possible.

A stout, jovial man with long black curls and a grinning face approaches us with his native Samoan greeting.

"Tālofa! Tālofa! Hello, my friends! A beautiful scarf for a beautiful..."

He stops and squints at me, then nods his big round head knowingly. He looks to Damon, and says,

"Lē tūmau."

Damon looks at the man with a wary eye, and says, "Pardon?"

"The name of the island," I acknowledge, "so, what of it?"

"No, I mean yes, but also you... *Lē tūmau.*" He bobbles his head as if we are in perfect understanding of one another, then to Damon he says, "She is... how I can say to you? She is transient." Then to me, "Ioe? Yes?"

I look at Damon, alarmed and unsure. He gives a small shrug, then nods. Strange times call for acceptance of strange conversations. I turn my gaze to the man.

"How did you... do you..."

"My name is Fetu," he interrupts. "Did it happen here, on the island?"

"I— yes. It did."

"Ah ha. Well, I suppose you are looking for your helper, then?"

"My..."

"Your helper. The one who guided you over."

A derisive snort escapes from my mouth.

"Uh, yeah, some guide he was. He just told me to jump. Then the little shit was gone."

Fetu laughs, his big belly bouncing. When he sees the grim look on Damon's face, he stops. Or at least slows considerably.

"Oh, my friend, fa'amalie atu. I'm sorry, for you, this isn't at all funny. I suppose you came here looking for answers."

We both give him an emphatic nod.

"Okay, well, I hope you get what you came for, then."

"Wait. That's it? Can't you— I don't know, tell me where this kid is, at least?"

"Fa'amalie atu. I can't."

"Can't? Or won't?"

"Whoa, whoa, don't shoot the shopkeeper, lady. I *can't* because I don't know. Those guys come and go as they please, you know? They don't, like, check in with us stayers.

Damon and I look at each other, confused.

"They? Stayers? I don't understand anything you're saying. I — *we* need you to explain what's happening to me."

"Like I said, I *can't*. Just try to relax. Enjoy the island. I'm sure you'll get your answers, okay?"

He inches away, glancing around as if looking for an escape hatch. I'm not ready to let him go, but Damon puts a hand on my arm.

"Birdie, let him get back to work. He's helped us enough for now. Come on, let's go for that walk."

I drag my feet, but let him lead me away, back into the sunshine. Damon is bracing himself for my tirade just as surely as I'm building up to one.

"I mean, what was that?"

"Well, Birdie, I…"

"*I can't tell you*," I mimic, "pu-lease. Obviously, he knows what's going on."

"Not necessa…"

"*Relax*, he says. Relax? Who is he to tell us to relax? What did he call me again? Transient? I'll give him..."

"Birdie! Stop, please."

Damon takes my arms and gently but firmly pulls me close to him, pressing his forehead against mine, and waiting until I sufficiently calm down before trying to speak again.

"Yes, sweetheart. He knows something, but it's not for him to tell, I guess. Let's do what we said we were going to do, okay?"

I nod, not convincingly.

"Birdie. *Be in the moment.* Remember? Let's not waste our moments being frustrated. The answers will come…or they won't."

Inhale, exhale. I breathe in his words, his tone, his scent. I'm centered again. I nod, now a little more convincingly.

"Okay. Let's do this."

SEVENTEEN
CAGES

What do you want? You want the moon?
Just say the word and I'll throw a lasso
Around it and pull it down.
George Bailey, It's A Wonderful Life

Once, when we were first dating, I dragged Damon into a pet store. There were angora rabbits in the window, and I wanted to hold one. Inside, I pointed to the first one I saw. It was a snow-white ball of feather-soft fur with a black circle around one eye. I asked the girl behind the counter if I could hold him.

"He's like Petey from The Little Rascals! Isn't he precious?"

I tried to get Damon to hold the rabbit. He refused, his arms crossed over his chest and only glancing quickly at the rabbit before looking away. Heat rose in my chest, across my face.

"Oh, my God. You don't like animals? How can you *not* like animals?" I asked, my eyes wide.

"I like them very much."
"Then hold it."
"No, thank you."
"Why not?"
"Because."
"Because *why*?"

The heat in my face was now furnace hot, the girl twisted the strings of her apron and looked away. Damon was unwavering in his refusal. Embarrassed, I handed the rabbit back over to the girl and stormed out of the pet shop, Damon in tow.

We'd been on our way to the coffee shop, three doors down, and continued there without another word. Without looking at each other, we placed our orders and took them to a table outside. My cheeks still tingling, I made a project of pulling the cardboard sleeve from my coffee cup, ripping it into little corrugated strips, and flicking them onto the table. He sipped his coffee, watching me.

"You're angry. Why?"
"I'm not."

Rip. Flick. Rip. Flick.

"Yes, you are. Don't play games. You're angry because I didn't want to hold the rabbit?"

I shrugged.

"You felt embarrassed in front of the girl."

A statement, not a question. That he knew this, this secondary layer to my feelings, and articulated them with ease and understanding...well, I wanted to cry. He sighed, set his cup down, and reached across the table to still my hand mid-flick.

"And the only thing you hate more than being embarrassed is crying."

I gave a curt nod, studying my mess of cardboard shreds intensely.

"I'm sorry I caused you to be embarrassed. Birdie, I love animals. I didn't want to hold the little guy because I'd get attached. I don't want to get attached because I can't bear to keep anything in a cage."

I looked up at him then, a slight crease forming between my brows, a smile twitched at my lips.

"I know, I know. Maybe I'm ridiculous. Maybe they don't know anything is wrong. But, imagine spending all your life in a cage? Never being free? It's just... it's cruel. I can't."

"What about fish?"

"Nope. Can't do it. Not when there are oceans or lakes or rivers they can be in."

Oh, my. This man is mine.

My icy tone completely thawed, my embarrassment abated, and my ego checked.

"Damon Michael Harrison, you are all kinds of amazing, you know that? I'm sorry, I misjudged that whole thing. I misjudged *you*."

"Was that our first fight?"

"I think it was."

We laughed, we were us again.

I smile, recalling that day.

"What's that smile for, Birdie?"

We're walking along the beach, our backs to the cliffs.

"I was remembering our first fight."

His forehead crinkles as he tries to remember, then he chuckles.

"The rabbit?"

"You remember."

"Like it was yesterday. What made you think of that, anyhow?"

I shrug. At a loss for words just like I was on that day, although not out of anger or embarrassment this time.

"Are you replaying our life in your head?"

I nod.

"Me too," he nods back.

"We've never had a fight worse than that. Is that strange? Don't answer, it doesn't matter. I guess I'm just thinking about how much good stuff we've filled these five— now six— years with. We've shared something that some people have looked for their whole lives, and never found."

"We are the lucky ones, aren't we Birdie?"

Despite our current circumstance, he says this with no irony, only sincerity. And I fully agree. All the anger and resentment are gone. Completely. We *are* the lucky ones. Nothing that has happened can change this. My dying wasn't anything but life happening. *It's your time*, said the boy.

"Damon?"

I stop him. He looks down expectantly at me, with pure love in his eyes.

"I have loved you too, from the moment I saw you in the bookstore. I have loved every moment of our life. I hope you have always known how profoundly I have loved you."

Romantic declarations have never been 'my thing.' But I put *everything* I have into these words. And he hears them, to the bottom of his soul. I know that he does. If he ever once wondered, he'll do so nevermore. I know this, because for the first time ever, Damon is rendered speechless.

He takes my face between his hands, tucks my hair behind my ear, kisses my forehead, my eyelids, my cheeks, my mouth. His tears mingle with mine. We are not sad, we are joyous. Love is the key to eternity, and we hold it. From behind Damon, a young voice calls out.

"Hello, lady. You have been looking for me, yes?"

EIGHTEEN
AZRAEL

I know there'll be a time for you and I Just take my hand and run away Think of all the pieces of the shattered dream We're gonna make it out someday We'll be coming back Coming back to stay When the night comes
—When the Night Comes, Joe Cocker

The boy is as beautiful as I remember. His amber eyes watch me with something like bemusement. The Samoan has told him what I said. *The little shit.* The recollection makes me cringe a little now.

"Damon? Do you…"

"Yes, I do."

He takes my hand and pulls me close to his side. Not yet, that handhold says.

"Hello, Mister."

"Hello, kid. What's your name?"

The boy smiles, a straight row of wide, grown-up white teeth set in his child's mouth. He is only a boy at this moment, nothing more. I start to think, *maybe that's all he ever was*, but then…

"I am called Azrael."

There is no ambiguity, no attempt at deception or suspense. He is an angel of death, so says his name alone. I'm neither frightened nor relieved. I suppose the word for what I feel right now is: *validated*.

Damon nods beside me.

"So now what?" Damon says.

The boy looks puzzled for a moment as if he's been asked to solve a curious riddle. Then he shrugs and gives us a beguiling smile.

"What do you want?" he asks.

"What do we *want*? What kind of question is that?"

The flash of anger in Damon's tone causes the boys smile to falter, but only for a second. He bobs his head once, twice.

"Oh, I see. You think this is a trick or something, right Mister? No trick. Tell me what you want."

He says the last sentence with slow emphasis. Azrael looks from Damon to me, then back again. His expression is patient but encouraging. Like he's saying in his mind, '*come on, now, you know what to ask, you* know.' But we don't. At least *I* don't.

What I do know, or what I *think* I know, is that the Angel of Death is no more or less than that. He takes, he does not give. So, is this a cruelty, a tease, or a joke to be asking us what we want? Just so he can say, '*sorry, no can do, my friend*?' As if reading my mind, which I suppose he can do, he says,

"Oh, not you Miss Birdie. *Mister*. What does Mister want? Think carefully, Mister."

"My name is…"

"No. Do not tell me your name until you know what you want. I'm sure you know, but I can wait. I have time."

He smiles when he says this, but it is not the sinister, menacing grin one would expect from the Angel of Death. It is sweet, open, genuine. I see he has no malice or ill intent. He has a job to do, and he simply does it. The boy turns to leave, but I stop him.

"Wait! What do you mean, '*you think you know what Damon wants*?' Does that mean you can…?"

"No, Miss Birdie. I cannot do that. It is like you said, 'I can take, not give.' Nothing more, nothing less."

"I didn't say…"

"You didn't have to."

Again, the shrug of those pointy dark shoulders, flash of a winsome smile. Damon smiles back at him, but his eyes, they do not smile along with his lips. He and the boy have had some exchange that I am not privy to, but there is a spark of fear alighting on the edge of my mind.

"Damon, what…"

"Let's continue our walk, Birdie." To the boy, he says, "We will see you later, friend."

"Yes, you will."

He says it in the same way someone would tell you the day of the week. Matter-of-factly.

Damon takes my arm and turns me away from Azrael, but I can't help but look back. I half expected him to have vanished, but no. The boy, wearing swim trunks (*same as last year*) walked barefoot and casual along the shoreline. Stopping to examine a shell, then tossing it back to the ocean.

Just a boy. Just a boy. Just a boy, I tell myself. Another couple is walking towards him. When they are within a few feet of Azrael, they make a wide arc around him, though they don't look at him.

A toddler runs up to the water near him, then stops and begins crying. His mother scoops him up in her arms, checks him for injury, and in finding none, tickles him until he giggles with glee. They never look at the boy beside them. But he watches them. Azrael is aware of my stare, looks up and smiles, raising his hand in a quick wave as he does. I don't wave back, but instead, allow Damon to pull me away.

We are quiet as we walk. The gulls cry and swoop low around us. The waves are gentle today. They roll in cool and smooth, lapping at our bare feet. Our hands are clasped, and Damon swings our arm just as he'd done the day we met, as he's always done. He is relaxed, at peace. More so than someone who's just met the Angel of Death should be. I am alarmed by this, but I don't know why.

"Everything is fine, Birdie. Everything *will* be fine. Trust me, okay?"

"But, what…"

"Shhh, babe. Look, dolphins."

A pod, surprisingly close to the shore, frolic, and race. He watches until they are out of sight. I watch them too. But mostly, I watch Damon. The sun is heading towards the west, catching his profile in its glow. His eyes are shining amber and gold, fine lines at the corners that deepen when he smiles. The bristle along the jawline of his unshaven face is russet and dark blonde, but with a fleck of silver now more plain than ever.

"I just want to grow old with you," I sigh.

He blinks hard, then takes my hand without looking at me. His jaw clenches, unclenches. His temple pulses with each. Looking down at the sand, he nods his head. We had it all planned out, over sushi and wine one night, three years ago. Or rather, *he* had it all planned out.

...

Waving his chopsticks over his sashimi, Damon painted a picture of our future in bright, bold colors and wide strokes. He was working hard at distracting me, *us*, from our private grief.

"And, Birdie, you— your hair will be as long as it is now, but silver. You'll wear wide brim hats in your garden, and force me to drink tea in the afternoon..."

"I suppose you'll look as virile and handsome as you do now, and not have gone bald and paunchy?"

I try to say this teasingly and light, it comes out flat, hollow.

"Of course, silly."

He's trying, though the rapport is notably one-sided.

"And will I have fifty cats and give them people names? Isn't that what women who can't..."

I choke on the rest. I couldn't look up from my dim sum, either. My chin wouldn't stop its damn quivering. Damon dropped his chopsticks to the table and grabbed my hand. He knew better than to ask me to look up. He knew I couldn't, not yet. He knows me by heart.

"Sweetheart, don't. Don't think that way. Whatever happens, no matter what *happened*, it will always, *always* be us. Be sad, be heartbroken... I am, too. *We* are. Just don't... please don't pull away from me, okay? I need you, Birdie."

He knew I was folding inward. Falling. Drifting away from him, rejecting him. It was no fault of his, only mine. *I* failed. *I* miscarried. *Miscarried.* I hated that word. It says, to me, I did it wrong, incorrectly. My body did not protect our baby, did not hold and carry her *right*. I lost her. Fourteen weeks. The size of a lemon. She could squint, frown, and suck her thumb. Tiny hands and feet, moving and kicking. And though I couldn't feel her yet, I could *feel* her. She was there, and then she was not.

The only thing greater than the irrational shame I felt at failing my biological job, was the indescribable sense of loss. She wasn't just a - a *fetus*, she was a life that was envisioned and imagined over dinners and late—night marathon conversations. She was bows and dresses. Pretty pink floral wallpaper, pre-school and college. First dances and soccer games, tennis lessons and a new puppy to grow up with. She was going to be our world. She was our plan.

That night in the restaurant marked one month since I'd lost our baby. Damon had been treading cautiously around me. I was glass, I was fragile. Sharp edges and hard lines. Painfully thin, unreadable, unreachable. Something he'd never seen me be before. I was a stranger to him, and to myself. I hated that face in the mirror, I hated my inability to be okay. *Be okay, damn it,* I willed myself. Then I'd slept for two days.

I tried to deny her realness. She wasn't a *baby* yet. She couldn't have survived outside of me yet. Then the tidal wave slammed into me again, and I was dragged down by the undertow. They say never fight the current, so I didn't. I let it pull me away, away, away. Away from Damon. Away from me. No one else knew I couldn't. Just couldn't.

That night in the Japanese restaurant on the corner of Beaumont and Lester, four words pulled me back to shore.

I need you, Birdie.

I looked up then, through the two fishbowls of unshed tears to see Damon drowning, too. The tide was trying to take him away as well, but he was fighting. He was fighting for us, and I'd left him alone to do it. I blinked. Two fat tears splashed on the table and my vision cleared. I could see my Damon clearly again.

My heart — friend and foe that it is — filled with fierce love for the angel of a man across from me and I decided right then to be okay.

"You will have grey hair as well, unruly as it is now, with a trim beard to match and a cane, though you won't really need one. You'll have decided it makes you look distinguished. You'll try to take up a pipe. But I quash the notion before you could light the first one. So instead, you'll just carry it around in your shirt pocket as if you *might* smoke it, given the whim."

He smiled, relief erasing every line on his face. His Birdie had come back to him. We bantered back and forth the whole night, closing down the restaurant and then walking home in the rain. We were changed, but okay.

...

"Do you remember that night..."

"Yes, of course. I thought I'd lost you then."

"I know. You pulled me back, though. You knew how."

"You give me too much credit, Birdie. You always have."

"You've never given me a reason to feel otherwise."

"I'm glad. I hope I've never let you down. That would..."

"You haven't. Ever. I don't know how many people get to say that about their partner, but *I* get to. I like to think we would've survived anything that came our way."

"What about...."

I know what he's about to say before he says it. *Doug.* What about

"Doug."

"Yeah. I, uh, I can't even say his name without wanting to spit fire. How can you? How did... I need to know what happened."

I sigh, take a deep breath. And I tell him what happened. By the time I finish— it is not a long story— he is like a hurricane under glass. Contained, but barely. I wait. He paces. Throws rocks hard and far out to the depths of the ocean, grunting with the effort, until his arm is sore. Then he drops to his knees in the sand, gripping his hair in his hands, pulling it as if trying to yank the images from his mind.

This is when I go to him. I kneel in the sand before him, gently take his hands down and compel him to look at me. There's nothing to say, not with words. If we never spoke another sentence, it would be no loss, for we know *everything* there ever is to say to one another.

Later, as we are walking back to the hotel, he says,

"Thank you."

He is thanking me for not telling, and for telling. He is thanking me for our life, our love.

"Thank *you*," I answer back.

NINETEEN
BLUEPRINTS

*"Overcome space, and all we have left is Here.
Overcome time, and all we have left is Now."*
— Richard Bach, Jonathan Livingston Seagull

When I was twelve, I had my first big crush. His name was Danny Pascarella, a neighborhood kid. He was fourteen, and he played the drums. I thought he was perfect. Danny had shoulder-length, dark, straight brown hair that hid eyes of the same color. He did this quick head flick kind of thing to get the hair out of his way. It was the cutest thing ever, as far as I was concerned.

After about a month of mooning over him — writing Danny + Taylor over and over in my notebook, talking about him incessantly to Aiden, and generally obsessing over his every move — Danny Pascarella finally noticed me.

"Hey, Taylor."

Oh, my God, oh my God, oh my God...

"Oh, hi Danny. I like your shirt."

"What? Oh, thanks. You like Van Halen?"

Nope, not at all.

"I love Van Halen. You, like, play the drums, or something, right?"

Thatagirl, play it cool.

"Yeah, that's right. Guitar, too. I can call you tonight, and you can listen to me rehearse if you want."

"Sure, I'd love to."

"Cool. What's your number?"

I gave him my number, and when he went back to playing basketball with his friends, I ran to Aiden's house to share the exciting news.

"Danny Pascarella? He asked for your number? Seriously?"

Aiden's suspicious, doubtful tone deflated my joy in an instant.

"Yes, *seriously*. Why?"

"Well, I'm just surprised. I thought he was going out with Tina Fulton. She's a Sophomore, you know. Better watch out, that's all I'm saying."

"They broke up, God. Can't you be happy for me?"

Aiden sighed dramatically and rolled his eyes.

"Yes, of course, I'm happy for you. I just know how it's all going to end, is all."

"Oh? And how's that?"

"With you crying into your pillow. Or on my shoulder. Or both."

Why did he have to go and ruin a perfect moment like that? All I could come back with was,

"Or maybe will go out and fall in love and be together forever. Why do you have to be so negative all the time?"

"That! That right there — that's why. We are twelve, Taylor. *Twelve*. Danny Pascarella is not your Prince Charming, trust me. He's a skinny boy with big teeth and in desperate need of a haircut."

"I love his hair. And shut up, Aiden. He's calling me tonight, so don't bother trying. We'll catch up on Dallas tomorrow."

"Oh, so now you're going to blow me off for this guy? We always watch Dallas on the phone together. You know what? Fine. Whatever."

"Fine!"

I stomped off. That night Danny did indeed call. I listened to him play the drums for an hour, then the guitar. When he finally got back on the line, it was to talk about his drums, his guitars, Eddie Van Halen, and his science test the next day.

This went on for about two months until I, at last, cleared the blinders away and decided that maybe Danny Pascarella wasn't all I'd imagined him to be. I'd like to say that Aiden had the decency to not say 'I told you so,' but he said that and more. We would repeat this pattern many, many times over the years.

Billy O'Brien. Jason Miller. Ian Summers. Brett whatever-his-last-name-was. Jerk I Almost Married Number One and Jerk I Almost Married Number Two. Different guys, same story. I was like the little bird in the story, Are You My Mother? Except I kept wandering around saying, Are You My Prince?

I met Damon two weeks to the day that I had told Aiden, in no uncertain terms, I was *done* looking for princes.

"Mhmm," he arched an eyebrow at me over his wine glass.

"I'm serious, Aid. Done. Fin. Finito."

"Sure, you are. You said that after Toad Number One, you know. And then you met Toad Number Two."

"What's wrong with me, Aiden? *Is* it me? It is, isn't it? Shit."

Aiden huffed, pressed his hands together, fingertips under his nose, and closed his eyes for a moment as he decided what to say, how to say it. I'd been crying on and off for days. Not because I missed Toad Two, it had already been months, and I'd been on some dates. I was thoroughly over him. I just wasn't over the disappointment.

"Okay, listen. You, sweetheart, are — and don't get all ego bloated — pretty, smart, and fun. You can hang with the guys, but they never forget you're a girl. You look like... who's that delicious blonde from Gossip Girl?" Not waiting for me to answer, "Blake Lively! Her, but like an older her. Oh, and with the personality of, like, Mary Tyler Moore. Mixed with Katharine Hepburn and Lucille Ball."

"Wow. Thanks, I think? So, what's my problem, then, if I'm... all that?"

"Your problem is, you give them the damn blueprint on day one. I mean, you practically give them a syllabus on Taylor 101."

I roll my eyes at him.

No, I don't. Shit. Yes, I do. Damn it.

"Well, I like to, I don't know, be honest. What's so wrong with that? It's like, *'here's me. Like it or leave it.'* I'm not sorry for being straightforward."

Aiden pinched the bridge of his nose, eyes closed. He then spoke as if I were a daft child.

"Tay. Honey. Sweetheart. You — and I say this with love, really, I do — you're an idiot. No, no, don't get all defensive. Put that angry eyebrow down. What I mean is, and bless your heart for never realizing it, you're *pretty*. The man-boys, they get all dopey eyed around you and tell you whatever you want to hear so you'll give them a chance. And you, you ninny, you don't make them work even the tiniest bit. *You give them the blueprint*, darling. Stop *doing* that."

He was right, of course. I did always give them the 'Taylor Blueprint.' A figurative mapping of exactly what to say and to do, how to be and how to act, should they be interested in me. It sounds conceited when I say it like that, I realize. *Perform these feats to be with me, the Great Taylor Tenley.*

No, it wasn't that way at all. The truth is, I've always felt like I was racing against time. That I needed to hurry up, pack all the moments in quickly before... well, turns out I was right. It was like a little voice inside my head whispered, *'find him, Taylor. Find him before it's too late.'* And I did. With only five years to spare.

Technically, Damon was a fluke. A stroke of luck, a fortuitous happenstance. Or fate, of course. But if my track record were the guide, he should've been just another toad. Another, *'you're not who I imagined you to be'*. I'd like to say I'd magically evolved after Toad Number Two, and that's why things happened the way they did with Damon and me. I'd be a liar, though.

I was still me, imagining princes around every corner, and sunsets with happily ever afters. When I saw Damon in the bookstore aisle, Hemingway in hand, I saw Prince Charming. I didn't tell myself, *'settle down, girl, he's just a guy holding a book.'* I thought, *'there you are.'* And there he was.

Granted, in that first year especially, I kept waiting for a toad to spring up in place of the too-good-to-be-true marvelous man that I was head over heels for. I *expected* it to happen. But it never did happen. He is still and always my Prince Charming.

We are back at the little café in the square. Fetu was at the front of his store, but when he sees us, he hurries back inside. He'd had about enough of me, it would appear. Still, I catch him glancing our way every time he comes out. The giant smile he wears for his customers falters then reappears.

"I suppose I should go over and apologize to Fetu."

"Who?" Damon asks.

"The shopkeeper. You know, the big Samoan."

"Oh! Him, yes. I'm sure he understands. After all, he knew right away what you…"

"What I am. Well, I'm glad *someone* does. *Transient.*" I harrumphed theatrically.

"What can I get you two?"

The waitress from this morning is gone, replaced by a young girl, no more than eighteen, with a long pony-tail and striking grey eyes. She has them trained on me for an especially long time, which is unusual because it's Damon the girls like to stare at typically.

"Hmm, not quite sure what I want yet. But I'll have a glass of Chardonnay to start, please. Wow, you have such beautiful eyes. I suppose you hear that a lot, though."

"Thanks, yeah, I guess." She shrugs.

After a few moments longer — too long, again — she turns to Damon, who's been waiting patiently with a small half-smile on his lips.

"Might as well make it a bottle, thank you."

A quick nod, then back to me. I blink at her, waiting. She opens her mouth, looks around surreptitiously, her eyes pausing where Fetu's shop is. I follow her gaze and catch Fetu himself looking back at her. He shakes his head once, then sees me staring and turns back inside.

"I-I'll bring you some waters while you decide on food. The, uh, salmon is really good."

I reach for her arm to stop her, but she's quicker. The grey-eyed girl is already across the café and behind the kitchen doors before I can say another word.

"What was that all about?"

"Damon, did you catch that exchange between her and Fetu? I think she was going to tell us something."

"I didn't see. Are you sure you do not just imagine things?"

"Really? You're kidding, right? I'm a dead woman that everyone can suddenly see. We're on an island where the Angel of Death apparently lives — in the body of a twelve-year-old, mind you —

and you're asking me if 'maybe I imagine' a strange moment that just occurred. Did we step into the Twilight Zone or something?"

"Touché, Birdie. You're right, sorry. You think she knows something about your... situation?"

"Yes, just like Fetu does. Damon, I think there are more, maybe even a lot more people like me here."

We both look around with a new appreciation of our surroundings. I study everyone in sight, as does Damon. A middle-aged couple sitting at the bar in matching Hawaiian print shirts. Three stools over, a younger man, maybe in his early thirties, with a full beard and sunglasses watching the television above the bar. The bartender, his silver hairline recedes into a thin pony-tail at the base of his neck, arms heavily tattooed in faded ink. The young couple from this morning.

They're sitting at a different table than earlier, looking less happy. She is whispering furtively at his downturned head as her eyes dart here and there suspiciously. Her eyes meet mine briefly, then she turns her chair away with a jerk. The metal legs scrape loudly, causing the handful of patrons to glance in their direction with varying degrees of surprise and annoyance. They all go back to their own universes.

What looked mundane moments ago, now looks suspect and curious. *Is* it my imagination? I think not. Our waitress returns, this time refusing to make any eye contact at all. She set the glasses down before us and pours the wine too fast, sloshing some of it on the table.

"Sorry." She mutters.

"No problem. So..." I look at her name tag, "Jaena, do you live on the island year-round?"

"I do now," she raises her eyebrows and widens her eyes as she says this.

"Oh, you're not happy about it?"

She shrugs, gives me a side eye.

"It could be worse, I guess."

"Do you have a family? On the island, I mean."

"No. Just me. Did you want to try the salmon? The grouper is pretty good, too."

"I — uh, sure. The salmon for me. Damon?"

He's been watching the girl, Jaena, throughout out the exchange, and leans in closer to her. He puts his hand on her arm, and she jumps away, then smiles apologetically.

"Not used to people..."

"Jaena?" Damon says, compelling her to look into his eyes. I hold my breath.

"What do you see when you look at my wife?"

"What? I— she... she's like me. We're...I'll go put your order in."

Abruptly she walks away again, forgetting to take Damon's order. But we don't really care about that, do we?

She's like me.

I look to Damon, questioning with my eyes what I think I'm beginning to partially understand, even if not why or how. He shakes his head, *I don't know, Birdie.* We drink our wine and hold hands across the table, but our eyes travel the cafe, the street. Both of us wondering, who of them are like me, and who are like him. *Why. How.*

A short while later, she returns. She is calmer now, more collected. Her full lips are set in a firm line, she has decided something, she is resolute. After she sets the two plates before us, she wipes her hands on the short waist apron, then wrings them together.

"Listen, I'm sorry about before — how I was acting. I'm just...this is all still pretty new to me, too. I-I'm like you. Or you're like me, I guess."

I nod, waiting for more.

"You're not surprised. Wow, you're faster than I was on the uptake. But I didn't have anyone with me to help. Not like him, at least."

She glances shyly at Damon, then back to me with her luminous eyes. There's a silvery scar on one eye, a scarlet one along her jawline. When she reaches for the bottle to refill our glasses, I see the scars on her wrist. *Oh, sweet girl.* I could be her mother. A young mother, but still, nonetheless.

"Tell me something, will you?" Damon asks her.

"That's the thing, I'm not *supposed* to tell you anything." She sighs, gets caught in Damon's puppy brown eyes, then says, "Okay, what?"

"Did you die here, on the island?"

We know the answer already.

"Yes."

"Jaena! Your order is up."

The cook, or maybe the owner of the café, calls in a warning tone from the other side of the kitchen door.

"Fine, I'm coming!" she calls back.

"Listen, good luck to you two, okay. I can't talk anymore, though, okay?"

She slid their bill across the table and never returned. The cook/owner himself came out after to take their payment, making it clear that he was in no mood for friendly conversation. Let alone the third degree.

When he walked away, we raised our eyebrows at each other with a laugh.

"Well, I guess that settles that, huh?" Damon chuckled.

"Yup, I guess so. What do we do now?"

"I think we should maybe go back to the hotel for a little while and, oh, I don't know, make wild passionate love in that king size bed."

"Why, Mr. Harrison! I am blushing!"

"Mrs. Harrison, I plan on making you do more than blush. Shall we?"

We practically run out of the café, forgetting all the peculiarities of the day, even if only for a little while. Back in the room, we make slow, playful love. Acting as if we have all the time in the world. It is Damon who acts this way and convinces me to slow down as well. *My* mind still says *hurry, get every moment in before it's gone.*

But Damon, he is leisurely. Every touch, every caress is deliberate and with presence. Each kiss from his lips, wherever they land, leave a ghost of him on my skin. His tongue tastes mine as if for the first time as if he must study and own it. His hips bear down, pause, pause, pause... and rise again. It's as if he has commanded time to wait for him, and time complies.

I allow myself to ride his wave of patience, giving over my doubt and worry to his calm confidence. I let him command me, us. I relinquish, give in and let his tide take me away.

When the heavy orange sun is but a couple of hours away from sinking into the ocean, we rise, shower, and dress again. We talk as married couples do...

'Did you pack my deoder— never mind, I found it."

"Babe, which one looks better? Blue? Or black?"

"Remember, it gets cool by the water. Grab a sweater."

We are *normal*. Damon and Birdie Harrison on vacation. The Harrisons at play. There is an undercurrent, of course. A conversation underneath the other one.

"What's going to happen?"

"I'm scared, Babe."

"I'm not ready to lose you again."

"What if..."

When we've finished taking turns in the long mirror, we stand in front of it together. Our eyes meet in the reflection. Damon's hands are on my shoulders, my hands are on my purse. We nod almost imperceptibly, he kisses the crown of my head and grabs the room key—card on our way out the door.

TWENTY
SCARS

The world breaks everyone, and afterward, some are strong at the broken places.
—Ernest Hemingway

Damon has a scar, a deep, crescent-shaped wedge of serrated flesh on his right shoulder blade. My fingertips have found and traced the spot many times. The first time, when we were exploring each other's bodies and committing them to memory, I asked him about it, how such a wound came about.

"Ah, that is a gift from Evan and Helena Harrison. Helena, specifically. They were having one of their infamous rows, as your beloved Brits would call it. I got caught in the crossfire."

He shrugged as if it were no big deal.

"And what the hell was the missile, geez? That's one hell of a scar. Whoever stitched it must've had their eyes closed, too."

"No stitches. That would've raised some eyebrows. Couldn't have that, now. Oh, and it was a glass ashtray. It was meant for my father's head, but Helena always had terrible aim. Especially when she was plastered."

"Jesus. How old were you?"

"Eleven."

"Wow, well, that kind of tops my fell-off-my-bicycle scar on my chin."

"Oh, Birdie, the stories I could tell you. But another day. I have a beautiful, blonde, naked woman in my bed with an adorable little scar under her chin, and I do not want to spend another moment talking about *my parents*."

"Yes, I suppose that is kind of creepy, hmm."

'Definitely. Let's play a game. You ready?"

"Umm, yes. I think."

"Peanut butter or Nutella?"

"Ahh, peanut butter," I laughed.

"Friday or Sunday?"

"Hmm. Sunday. No Friday. Wait…Sunday."

"Past or future?"

"Present."

"Good one, Miss Tenley."

"My turn. Ice cream or potato chips?"

"Ice cream."

"Oceans or Lakes?"

"Oceans."

"Fate or coincidence?"

"Fate."

"Lust or love?"

"Love. I love you, Birdie."

"I love you, too."

We still play this game sometimes. At night. In the dark. I wish we'd played it last night. Hoping we'll get the chance to play it tonight.

Down in the hotel lobby, a man plays the glossy black piano, an unfamiliar melody. It is sweet sounding, happy. We pass him by, Damon nods and smiles at him. He doesn't smile back, but he changes the tune mid key. Now he is playing something else. I recognize it instantly, as does Damon, even though it is slowed considerably.

"Did you..."

"No. Coincidence?"

"No."

We turn back, I take Damon's hand in both of mine. The pianist never looks up, but begins to sing in a low, halting voice...

"I can't...give you...

Anything...

But love...

Baby..."

It's beautiful and terrible all at once. I am mesmerized.

"Dream awhile, scheme awhile... we're sure to find...

Happiness...

And I guess..."

"Let's go, Birdie."

He gently, but firmly pulls me away. The man on the piano never looks up, but I know. He *sees* us. Me.

Though we're almost at the wide doors of the hotel and there are the sounds of other guests talking, mingled with rolling luggage carts and elevator dings, I still hear the one line above all else.

"You have to pay, kid...

For what you get, kid..."

I know that Damon hears it as well. His hand spasms around mine as if he'd just been stuck by a needle, but he doesn't look back. He starts walking faster.

"We can catch the sunset if we hurry," he calls over his shoulder.

I nod pointlessly; his eyes are trained ahead of him. *The sunset.* Everything feels like a metaphor. The piano keys, now only in my mind, sound jarring, discordant.

You have to pay, kid, for what you get, kid.

A sensation, like the flutter of a thousand butterflies, rises in my chest. Damon walks on, pulling me along with him as I lag behind.

"Damon! Wait. Please. I- I need a moment."

He whirls around, grabs ahold of my arms above my elbows in an insistent grip.

"We're running out of time, Birdie. We have to hurry. He's waiting."

"Waiting? He..." Of course, I know who he means, "you mean Azrael. What's happening, Damon? What are we doing?"

"I'm not sure."

But he cuts his eyes away when he says this. Damon has never been a good liar. He is lying to me now.

"Yes, you are. Why are you in such a hurry to meet him? What exactly are we running out of time for?"

His eyes are wide, pleading. His grip on my arms almost painful. I am panicked, he is afire with excitement. I take two fistfuls of his shirt and pull him in. His arms wrap tightly around me, pinning my arms between us. He pulls back just enough to let my arms drop to his waist, then takes my head between his hands.

"Birdie, don't you see? I was supposed to jump with you. I *am* supposed to jump with you."

I search his face, then suddenly understanding dawns.

"Damon, no. *No.* You are not jumping. I can't let you do that. I *won't*."

I try to say it with force, but my voice shakes, betraying me. He smiles down at me as if I've said something sweet.

"Don't you want to spend forever with me, Birdie?"

Damn him.

"It's not about what I want Damon. Azrael gave you a *choice*. It wasn't a command, it was a choice."

"Yes, and I choose you. I always have, I will always choose you."

I ignore his protestation, break away from his hold.

"This is insane, Damon. Do you hear what you're saying? How do you even know that's what he's offering?"

"I…"

"You *can't* know! And where is he, even? For all we know, he's gone, off stealing someone else's life away!"

People are beginning to look at us with quick side glances, then giving us a wide berth. I let Damon take my arm again, and we walk; slower this time. Damon's impatience propels him forward. My hesitation is like an anchor dragging along the seabed.

"You're right, I don't know. Not for certain at least. But I think that is what he meant. And I also think that he's just waiting for us to come to him."

"Oh? And how are we supposed to know where to find him? Telepathy?"

"You know where Birdie. You've known all along."

I stop again, halting Damon in his tracks. We look up at the thing I've been avoiding since we pulled into the marina. They have been hard to miss, those imposing, looming natural wonders of rock and earth. Their jagged faces and jutting chins compel our eyes to take in their magnificence. It is where I met the boy who brought me death. It is the cliffs.

TWENTY-ONE
JUMP

You jump, I jump, remember?
—Jack, Titanic

The last time I climbed a tree (or any unsecured height, for that matter) I was sixteen. So stupid. Billy O'Brien, possible prince of the month, dared me. I never met a dare I could turn down, unfortunately for me.

"I am too a tomboy. Always have been, thank you very much."

"No way, Tenley. You're a girlie girl, I can tell by looking at you."

"Oh, shut up, Billy. What do you know?"

"I know you can't climb a tree."

"Oh, really? Says who?"

"Says me. If you're such a tomboy, then climb that willow over there and prove it."

He cut his eyes and jerked his peach-fuzzed chin in the direction of lone Weeping Willow tree at the edge of the park. There was a bench underneath it. The royal blue paint chipped and faded away to reveal the weathered wood underneath. Someone had spray—painted 'Patti + Jeff 4ever'on the backrest.

Shit. Why did I tell him that? I haven't climbed a tree since I was nine.

"Sure, no problem."

Well, it was a problem. I sprinted over to the bench, hopped up and grabbed the lowest hanging limb. I had my right leg almost over when the branch shimmied once and then, with a loud crack, broke away from the tree. My fall was less than graceful and probably would have been funny had I not whacked my chin on the edge of the bench.

Embarrassed, I tried to jump up quickly, and give a little 'oops' shrug. But as soon as I started to say, "I'm fine', there was a rush of heat at my chin, and something dripped. I cupped my hands underneath it. Blood, bright red and pooling in my hands.

Billy's eyes became saucers, and his face paled. For Christ's sake, he was going to faint. Instead of rushing to my side and offering the bandana in his back pocket to stop the flow, he covered his eyes.

"Oh shit, oh *shit*, Taylor. I'm gonna be sick."

'Oh, calm down, you idiot. Drive me to the walk-in clinic. I'm going to need stitches."

"Stitches? Shit. Wait, you're gonna bleed all over my car!"

"You know what, Billy? You're an ass. Just go. I'll call Aiden."

"Are you-you're sure. Cuz I…"

"Go, Billy."

And he did. Proving without a doubt: he was definitely *not* my prince.

It's not Billy I'm thinking about as I look out over the cliff, not really. Not his cowardice or insensitivity, his unprincelike behavior. It's the tree, or rather the climb that rests on my mind. I realize now, it's not the *heights* I hate. It's the falling. There's the age-old saying, 'It's not the fall I fear, but the landing.' But that's not what I mean. Falling is a reminder that we can't fly. I want to *fly*. Soar, ascend. Pull out the thesaurus, add them all.

For as much as I've always had recurring nightmares, I've had a recurring flying dream. So, when I wasn't having terrible images of drowning, I dreamt of flying. One moment standing at the edge of a thing— a staircase, a cliff, a building. The next falling forward, arms outstretched. The air would catch me in an embrace and lift me, carry me away. Over fields and buildings, lakes and rivers. Sometimes fast, other times slow. It was effortless. I didn't need to flap my arms or kick my legs, the wind supported me.

Staring out past the alcove to the sea I wonder, if I knew then what I know now, would I have imagined myself flying instead of falling when I fell from this very cliff? I pose the query to Damon, who is sitting knees bent and back against a boulder, watching the sky, watching me, and for one of the very few times ever, he is puzzled by my question.

"I'm just wondering, is all. I'm thinking about the things we'd do differently if given a redo."

"Then I suppose it's been a good life if you can only come up with choosing to... die differently, hmm?"

"Yes... and no. I would never change a moment of my life. Every step, every *mis*step brought me to you. One little change could've altered the course of everything. And I don't suppose we have much say about how or when we die. But I if I'd realized it — that I was dying — I'd like to think I'd have embraced it."

Damon says nothing to this. I suppose he's trying to wrap his mind around embracing death when there's so much of life to be desired.

"I'm not explaining it well, am I?"

"I understand, I think. It's because you, *we* learned that death isn't an end. We don't have to be afraid of it. We can...fall into it without dread. Close?"

"Yes, exactly. Except I don't want to fall, I want to fly."

Damon's eyes the horizon, now glowing in the last of the sun's set. His jaw works, his brows furrow, then, as if he's come to some decision, he nods.

"Fly, huh? Flying sounds nice, Birdie. What do you say we fly together?"

"Damon, you..."

"Hello, friends! You are here. I was beginning to wonder if you would come."

It is the boy, come as Damon knew he would. *Azrael has come for me.*

TWENTY-TWO
FLY
Trouble tied to a feather/ I feel a little bit better.
—Feather, The Lone Bello

"You knew we'd come, Azrael."

The boy smiles at Damon and then lets a burst of boyish laughter tumble out his mouth. As if Damon has told him a joke and he's a moment slow on the uptake. Damon smiles back but does not laugh even though the sound is the contagious kind.

"Yes, I suppose I did, Mister."

"You also know I've made my decision, don't you?"

Azrael does not answer him but instead turns to me.

"And what say you, Miss Birdie?"

I stride over to where Damon is and place myself between him and Azrael and fold my arms across my chest.

"No."

"No? You have surprised me, Miss. Don't you want..."

"What I *want*, is to go back. Undo *this*."

I turn my hands in, towards my body, and wave them up and down. Azrael tilts his head and furrows his brows at me, then his eyes soften as he gives a small nod of his dark head. A small swell, a rising in my chest. *He's going to let me come back.* Then he speaks, not to me, but to Damon, who has risen and stands behind me.

"What is your name, Mister?"

"No!"

It bursts from my throat and out of my mouth before Damon can say his name aloud. I whirl around and grab his wrists tightly as if he's trying to move rather than speak. My eyes search his, they gaze down softly into mine. He raises one hand, mine still wrapped around his wrist and smooths my hair, tucks it behind my ear. I lean my face instinctively against his palm.

"Birdie, don't you see? *This* is what's meant to happen, to *have* happened. It's why we've been led back to Tumau. The very name of the island is the answer."

I step out of his touch, away from his words, and risk a glance at the boy. He has turned his back to us and overlooks the sea. Wrapping my arms around my body, I shiver from a sudden chill in the air. The sun has nearly sunk into the ocean and the sky, approaching twilight, is streaked with crimson and orange, indigo and pink.

"No one else had ever heard of the island," I say softly. "When I mentioned to my mother and father— they said they'd never heard of it."

"Neither had Charlie or Jack, Mel or..."

Doug. He didn't need to finish. I struggle to recall how or when *we'd* heard about the island.

"Birdie, we *are* getting a chance to undo this... just not the way we'd imagined."

"Do you even hear what you're saying? What you're *suggesting*? Damon, it's crazy. It's *wrong*. You can't...I can't let you..."

My voice breaks, it won't let me say: *kill yourself.*

"Miss Birdie, Mister... time is running out. I will need your answer. Now." After a pause, he added, I am sorry."

At his words, Damon is mobilized. He takes my hand in his and practically pulls me over to the cliff's edge, alongside Azrael. Though his heart must be beating thunderously, his hand is surprisingly dry.

How can he not be terrified?

As if reading my thoughts, "I'm not afraid, Birdie. I'm ready for forever. *Our* forever. Do you trust me?"

I trust him more than myself. I always have. I always will. On the breeze, a snowy white feather drifts before me. Instinctively, I open my palm to it, and it tickles my flesh. Closing my eyes, I make a wish and blow it away again. My head nods, almost imperceptibly. But Damon sees it.

Azrael, now beside Damon, clears his throat delicately. He is waiting. A cool breeze ripples through our hair. Damon has reclaimed my hand, and I'm not cold anymore. His calm seeps through his palm into mine, and I force myself to breathe slowly.

I look only at him. His face in profile is more beautiful than ever. Serene. Certain. His strong jaw softened now with the shadow of a light beard, is set firm and his back is straight. A peaceful smile rests on his lips as his thumb caresses the side of my hand. His chest rises and swells with a deep breath, and he closes his eyes he tips his head back as he releases it. His tranquil smile remains.

"Are you ready for forever, Birdie?"

"Yes. Are you sure..."

Damon takes my chin between his thumb and finger and tilts my face up to his. Then leans down and brushes his mouth against mine before whispering,

"I am."

We kiss, not as two saying goodbye, but hello. Azrael shuffles a bit and toes the dirt, coughs once.

"Yes, yes. I know, you're waiting. Very well, kid. My name is Damon Michael Harrison..."

STILL HERE

THE END

ABOUT THE AUTHOR

Elsa Kurt is a multi-genre, indie & traditionally published author, brand designer, and speaker. She currently has six novels independently published, as well as three novellas published with Crave Publishing in their Craving: Country, Craving: Loyalty, and Craving: Billions anthologies. She is a lifelong New England resident and married mother of two grown daughters. When not writing, designing, or talking her head off, she can be found gardening, hiking, kayaking, and just about anywhere outdoors. Or, you could just find Elsa on social media:
https://facebook.com/authorelsakurt/
https://instagram.com/authorelsakurt/
https://twitter.com/authorelsakurt
https://www.goodreads.com/author/show/15177316.Elsa_Kurt
https://allauthor.com/profile/elsakurt/
https://amazon.com/author/elsakurt
and her website, http://www.elsakurt.com